The Surrender of Persephone
By Selena Kitt

Dedication

To the man who moves in geological time, you are my rock.
I couldn't have done it without you.

Prologue

"Mother!" Persephone rolled her eyes and flipped her long, honey-colored hair over her shoulder. "I'm not a child anymore!" She fingered the delicate golden heart dangling on a thin chain between her breasts, frowning as she opened the locket. It contained some magic Hephaestus had forged for her mother, with images of her and Demeter on either side. Persephone didn't want to seem ungrateful, but this was too much!

Demeter just smiled at her daughter and continued to separate the wheat from the chaff with quick, deft movements. "I know, darling. I just worry about you. Mothers worry. It's what we do."

"Don't you trust me?" Persephone crossed her arms over her chest.

"It's not you I worry about." Demeter's eyes narrowed just slightly as she gazed out the open window into the bright summer sun. "It's them."

"Them?" Persephone turned her head to look across the field, not at all recognizing the lurking monsters her mother clearly perceived. She just saw flowers and trees and a world full of brightness and exciting possibility. "Do you mean…men?"

"Men." The older goddess spat the word, tucking a white-blonde strand of hair behind her ear, leaving golden pieces of wheat there. "They are never to be trusted. Men only want one thing."

Rolling her eyes again, Persephone went to the window and leaned against the ledge with a sigh. She had heard this lecture too many times to count and knew it by heart. Demeter spoke, but the young goddess didn't listen. Instead, she stared off into the distance and dreamed about faraway lands, handsome strangers, and daring adventure. The chain around her neck was supposed to keep her safe from the hands of men, but Persephone wasn't so sure she wanted to be kept safe. Fingering the heart, she wondered what magic made it work.

She tuned back into her mother's voice: "…even your own father, Zeus himself, has taken maidens at his whim. You are my only daughter, Persephone. You can't understand how precious you are to me."

Persephone gritted her teeth and closed her eyes for a moment, glad her mother couldn't see her face. Then she had a thought. "What happens if I lose it?"

"It's an unbreakable chain," Demeter explained. "Hephaestus promised me it would keep you safe."

"But how does it work?" the young goddess insisted, turning the heart over in her fingers.

"It's imbued with a mother's love." The older goddess approached her daughter, wrapping her arms around Persephone's waist from behind and resting her chin on the girl's shoulder. "Do not seek to test it. I promise you, it will keep every man who seeks to defile you at bay."

Just what I need, Persephone thought as her mother's lips pressed her cheek. *Yet another restriction on my freedom.* She had never been with a man and, thanks to her mother, hadn't had the opportunity to meet many of them. Still, the ones she had chanced upon had struck her as…very interesting.

Of course, she couldn't tell her mother. Instead, she turned and hugged Demeter, kissing the older goddess' dry cheek. "Thank you, Mother. I'm supposed to meet Artemis and Athena in the meadow."

Demeter moved back and let her daughter go, still smiling. "I'd tell you to be careful…but I don't have to any longer!"

Persephone didn't answer as she shut the door behind her and started walking down the pathway into the woods. Beyond the thick huddle of trees, she knew Athena and Artemis would be waiting. Maybe she should talk to them about it. They might have some deeper wisdom to share.

She found herself so lost in thought she didn't notice the hand reaching out to tug at the back of her robe. Turning, she found herself face-to-face with a man.

"Ah, there is the delectable Goddess of Spring!" His voice rumbled low in his barrel chest, and his smile lined deeply at the corners. His salt-and-pepper hair and beard showed his human age clearly. "You will be pleased to make my acquaintance, young Persephone. I am Pirithous, King of Lapiths, Argonaut extraordinaire!"

"You startled me!" Persephone took a step back, her hand at her throat. She wasn't used to people coming so close to her mother's cottage. Demeter's refuge remained hidden from human eyes, a secret to the world of men. *How did he find me and how does he know my name?*

"Your father has told me a great deal of you." Pirithous smiled warmly at her, reaching for her arm. "There is no daughter of Zeus more worthy of my attention, so I hear."

Hesitating, Persephone glanced back and no longer saw her mother's home and knew Demeter couldn't see them, either. She touched the necklace at her throat and wondered how it was meant to protect her. Surely it would let her know if this man meant her harm.

"I am meeting friends." She nodded toward the field up ahead.

"You will love my kingdom." He went on as if she hadn't even spoken. "We are a fertile land, and I am a rich king. There are plenty of fields of flowers for you to pick, of course. When you aren't...otherwise occupied." His smile widened and he looped his arm through hers and began to walk. She stumbled after him, trying to keep up. "I had hoped to talk to your mother as well, but I couldn't resist telling you first."

"First?" She glanced up at him, puzzled.

"Yes." He slowed his pace to match hers, looking down at her. His eyes brightened and crinkled at the corners. "Persephone, you are the most beautiful daughter of Zeus. Certainly the most captivating and the one whom, you will be happy to hear, I have deemed the most worthy."

"Th—thank you." She flushed, swallowing hard. "Worthy of...what?"

"This is a lovely trinket." His thick fingers reached over to touch the locket around her neck. "But not nearly as beautiful as you, my dear." Looking down, Persephone frowned at the necklace. *It's supposed to protect me? Do I need protecting from this man?* "My own dear wife, Hippodamia, has passed on…" He sighed, his pace slowing even further as they made their way down the tree-lined path toward the field.

"I'm sorry to hear it."

"Yes, well, it leaves me wanting a companion." Pirithous stopped, taking both of Persephone's small hands into his. "And I find myself wanting you. There is none so worthy of my attention as you, goddess."

She blinked at him, still not understanding. *He can't possibly mean—*

"I came here today to ask you to be my bride, Persephone." He looked as if he were bestowing a great gift upon her, his chest puffed up, his chin proud.

Oh by the gods, he can't be serious! She stared, open-mouthed, and then—she couldn't help it—she laughed. The bright sound carried far. She covered her mouth with her hand to keep it from escaping, but it was no use. The thought she should marry this old man! Nothing short of someone telling her the world was round could have proved more ludicrous to her!

"I'm sorry…" Her apology disappeared in another gale of laughter. His face had turned a deep shade of red, his eyes narrowing to slits. "Forgive me. I didn't mean to offend you. It's just…just…" She burst into another fit of giggles.

"Do you believe yourself too good for me, young goddess?" His kind face turned into a terrible sneer. Persephone's laugh faded and she took a step back, bumping up against a tree as he advanced. "I may not be a god, but I am a king, and I more than deserve a wife who is the daughter of Zeus!"

"Please…" Persephone could back up no further, her back pressed against the trunk of the tree. Pirithous tilted her trembling chin up with his hand, his eyes blazing with hurt pride. "I didn't mean to—"

"You will be mine." His mouth crushed down on hers. Persephone struggled in his grasp as his meaty tongue forced its way past her teeth.

She beat at him and cried out in desperation, "Help! Mother!" Suddenly an incredible heat glowed against her chest and a blue flash burst from her locket. Pirithous flew backward from her with a cry of both pain and rage, clutching his heart. His shocked eyes met hers, and they both looked at the small bauble hanging from the chain around her neck. It now glowed blue around the edges.

"My mother gave me this." Incredulous, Persephone felt its heat when she lifted the locket in her hand. "For protection."

"I will have you!" His face twisted in anger as he struggled to his feet. When he lunged for her, they both saw the white-blue arc flare out from the necklace, strike him, and force him backward. She didn't wait for him to get up. Lifting the hem of her robe, she ran for the open field ahead.

Chapter One

Persephone sighed and tore another velvet petal off the daisy with a little more enthusiasm and vengeance than her mother probably would have liked. The Goddess of Spring should love picking flowers, not tearing them apart! It wasn't that she didn't like flowers, or sunshine, or brand new baby lambs. They were all wonderful—in moderation—but lately she had found herself with the urge to pull birds' nests out of trees and crush rose petals in her fists—not very Goddess of Spring-like behavior, to be sure. Of course, she hadn't done it, though the secret desire burned in her belly so often it began to scare her.

Persephone picked another daisy and tossed it into her basket, swinging it on her arm and glancing across the field. Athena and Artemis had promised to meet her and help her gather wildflowers for Demeter's Harvest Festival, but there was no sign of either of them yet. In the distance came the short, rhythmic report of someone chopping wood. She had been hearing it for half an hour and now cocked her head in that direction. Curious and decidedly bored, she slipped into the woods and followed the path toward the noise.

She touched the locket at her throat as she walked, glancing down to see if it glowed blue. It had been a week since Pirithous had confronted her in these woods, and the necklace had been quiet since. She had been too afraid to tell her mother about the incident, although she had relayed the details to Athena and Artemis. Both armed goddesses had prowled the perimeter of the meadow and pronounced the old man gone. Still, she tried to be more cautious than she had been before.

Slowing as she came closer to the source of the sound, she noticed a clearing near a small stream. A man—just a human, not a god—worked with an axe and some wood. He seemed to be making piles of it and Persephone wondered who he was and what the wood was for. She watched him lift his axe high above his head and bring it down to split a log.

Slipping behind a tree, she peeked around to see how the muscles in his back and chest rippled as he worked. Something about it made her long to touch his browned skin, and the thought made her flush.

The dark-haired man wiped his brow with the back of his hand, tossing the axe aside. He put his hands at the small of his back and arched with a groan. Glancing around the woods, he began to unfasten the loincloth he wore. Persephone stared, open-mouthed. She knew all about the differences between men and women, but had never seen a man completely naked before. The sight intrigued her.

The man waded into the stream up to his thighs, reaching down to splash water up over his hard, ridged stomach, and chest. He turned his back to her as he bathed, kneeling down in the water and wetting his hair, then shaking off the excess. Wanting a better view, she poked her head out a little further. The woodsman stood and stretched, and she found herself wishing she could see the path his hands trailed down the front of his body.

Persephone had been surrounded by feminine beauty all of her life, but her first glimpse of male beauty left her breathless and wanting more. She didn't think the responsive, aching throb between her thighs could get more intense until he faced her again and she saw his hand wrapped around his erection. Stunned by the beauty of his form as he stood in the middle of the stream, naked and glistening and touching himself, she felt her belly tighten with longing.

Fascinated, she saw his eyes close in pleasure, his hand moving faster and faster up and down his shaft. He had no idea she was there, his actions completely uninhibited. Persephone bit her lip, squeezing her thighs together against the pulse there. She knew what she was looking at. She had been taught about that masculine instrument of pleasure, made to deflower virgins, and she knew she should have been frightened. Instead she found herself excited and transfixed by the sight, her face flushed and her breath coming faster.

He threw his head back, giving a loud groan, and she watched, stunned, as his manhood erupted like a white hot geyser, shooting in thick, pulsing jets. She covered her gasp with her hand, her eyes wide as he spilled his pleasure into the stream.

The sight filled her with an incredible longing she had often felt but hadn't ever been able to identify before. *Will the ache between my thighs only be satisfied by a man?* she wondered as he sank down and relaxed into the stream again. Her mother had been grooming her since she could remember to be one of the virgin goddesses, like Athena and Artemis. *But what if I don't want to be a virgin?*

"Persephone!"

She whirled at the sound of her name, recognizing Artemis' voice at the edge of the woods. The man heard it, too, and before he discovered her behind the tree, Persephone took off running from a man for the second time in a week.

* * * *

Being between Athena and Artemis sometimes made Persephone long for the earth to open up and swallow her whole. It wasn't that she didn't enjoy their frequent little threesome romps in the flowering fields. Gods knew they pleased her in ways only two glorious goddesses could, but there was a self-sufficient detachment in them both that left her aching.

"Don't you ever want more?" Persephone rolled to her belly between them, swinging her delicate feet toward the sun's heat. She gazed at Athena through a gauze of flaxen hair, still tangled with the flowers they had been picking before they had thrown off their silken gowns, spread them wide, and sunk into a few blissful hours of divine pleasure.

"Didn't get enough, little one?" Athena chuckled. The deep resonance of her voice always surprised and scared Persephone a little. Or maybe it was the sword she always carried under her lustrous robes. Athena flicked one of her silky auburn curls over Persephone's freckled nose, making her sneeze.

"When is it ever enough for our precious Sephie?" Artemis laughed, leaning over to press a gentle kiss to the rounded swell of Persephone's exposed bottom. She rested her cheek there for a moment, still smiling, her dark hair tickling Persephone's thighs, making her wiggle and sigh. "Little beauty, don't you know we have everything?"

"What more could you want, really?" Athena asked. "We're goddesses. We can go anywhere. We can do anything." Athena stretched her long limbs and yawned. They didn't sleep or get tired, really, but they did get bored. Yes, they got bored a lot.

"That's not true..." Persephone stuck her tongue out at Athena's back. "We can't go everywhere." Athena's shadow blocked the sun and Persephone felt a chill.

"Where can't we go?" Artemis sat, too, her dark hair tumbling over her milk-white shoulders. She reached for her bow. Persephone always felt safe with them, tucked between two strong protectors, a sword on one side, a bow on the other. Alone, she sometimes felt liquid, like she could seep away into the earth and no one would even notice.

"Elysium..." Persephone propped her chin in her hand and gazed out across the field. "Imagine what the Elysian Fields must be compared to these...too good for even the gods..."

"Sephie!" Artemis pressed her fingers to the pout of Persephone's full lips. "By the gods, girl, pray Zeus didn't hear you! Ask swift Hermes, or perhaps dark Hecate. They are the only twain-travelers, and they do so at great cost. You do not want to go where shades go. There are darker things there than you have ever imagined..."

"Yes, precious," Athena assured her with a lopsided smile, leaning over to kiss her smooth cheek. "Even in your most rebellious dreams."

"Careful what you wish for, dearest." Artemis ran a slender finger down the length of Persephone's spine. "I think perhaps we should do something to dispel these terrible thoughts."

"Yes," Athena agreed, meeting the eyes of the dark-haired goddess over the blonde's bent head. "Something to take her mind off such things…"

"Ohhhh…" Persephone breathed a sigh, feeling two hands, one from each side, sliding between her tender, virgin legs and parting them. She closed her eyes at their touch, craving it, aching for more. Whenever they were together, it always seemed as if she could never get enough. She tried to commit it all to memory—the feel of their fingernails tickling the inside of her thighs, the brushing of their hair over her skin as they both leaned in, feathering kisses over the gentle curve of her behind.

Two trailing goddess tongues explored their way through her fleshy pink maze, making Persephone arch and moan in response. She didn't know who was doing what, and she didn't care—she just wanted more. Lifting her bottom high in the air, she wiggled toward them and reached between her own legs to open herself to their mouths.

"Eager, isn't she?" Athena murmured. Artemis chuckled in agreement as she crawled up beside Persephone on the grass.

"Oh don't stop…please!" Persephone pleaded, affirming the goddesses' opinions as she spread herself wider in offering to Athena's probing tongue. The little blonde's honeyed cleft parted at the redhead's insistence, and Persephone pressed the tender bud at the apex of her sex, showing Athena where she wanted her mouth.

The goddesses had long ago taught Persephone about the center of feminine pleasure—what they called the feminine omphalos, or "omi." Persephone had learned over time just how much delight her little omi could give, the goddesses always trying to find new ways to tickle each other.

Artemis wiggled her curvy form underneath the slender blonde, capturing Persephone's hungry mouth with hers. Persephone leaned into the dark-haired goddess' kiss, feeling the full lush press of her body, devouring her mouth as they squirmed together on the luxurious robes spread beneath them. Artemis' hands spread everywhere at once, her fingers slipping between them both to probe and spread Persephone's exposed sex, where Athena's tongue kept a delicious vigil on her sensitive omi.

Persephone's belly fluttered in response, and she moaned against the heavy globes of Artemis' breasts, sucking and licking eagerly, making her way to their big, brown centers as Athena's tongue worked its magic. Artemis gave a deep sigh, turning her attention to her own sex, the sweet rub of her hand sending sweet jolts of pleasure through Persephone as the goddess' large brown nipples began to harden under her attention.

Athena's mouth abandoned its pursuit between the young blonde's legs and Persephone whimpered, looking over her shoulder at the auburn-haired goddess, her eyes pleading for more. The redhead smiled, reaching for a handful of honey-colored curls and pulling Persephone up toward her.

"Oh!" Persephone's surprise was muffled by Athena's wet kiss, the goddess' mouth slanting across hers, giving back the sweet taste of her own honey as their tongues touched. Persephone, lost in the velvet softness of Athena's lips, straddled Artemis' rounded hips. The dark-haired goddess' fingers tweaked Persephone's nipples, making her moan against Athena's open mouth.

Persephone felt the heat of Artemis' sex against her own and rocked against it, longing to quench the fire between her legs. Athena chuckled, feathering kisses over the blonde's shoulder as she watched. The younger goddess struggled and moaned, trying to ease the tender ache.

"Like this…" Athena's hands moved over Persephone's thighs, moving her. Persephone responded to her guidance, slithering her body across Artemis, straddling her at an angle, so their legs made a delicious X, positioning their slick clefts as close together as possible.

"Oh yes…" Artemis' fingers stayed between them, spreading them both open. She put her knees up, rocking with Persephone as their juices smeared and blended together. Closing her eyes, Persephone ground her hips in circles, feeling the folds of the other goddess' flesh, all soft, tender pinkness, rubbing against her own.

Persephone tried to make their little omis kiss, lost in the slippery darkness of sensation, pressing her sex faster and faster toward release. Artemis' breath came more quickly as she pulled and tugged at her own nipples. Athena stretched out beside the dark-haired goddess and lifted one of her breasts. Artemis sighed as Athena drew it toward her mouth, licking the fat bud in the center, her lips closing fast around it and sucking.

Persephone cupped her own breasts, pinching and squeezing her nipples, sending additional little shocks of pleasure down to her pelvis. Artemis rolled like thunder underneath her now, moaning and meeting her with every pass. Persephone slid her hand down, feeling the wet squelch of them together, the slickness of their soft curls.

"Are you close?" Athena whispered against Artemis' nipple, flicking it with her tongue.

"Yes, oh yes!" Artemis squirmed against Persephone and grabbed her slim hips, rocking up to meet her. Persephone knew she wouldn't quite make it with her, but wanted to send the other goddess over. Knowing Artemis loved to be filled, Persephone slipped her hand down and found the goddess' slick entrance. Artemis gasped and bucked as Persephone probed, pressing her fingers into the sensitive flesh.

"Ohhhhhh!" Artemis moaned and Persephone felt the other goddess' climax in the muscles deep inside her slippery wetness, as if trying to rhythmically draw her fingers in further as the dark-haired goddess twisted and bucked. Persephone felt herself near the edge but wanted to hang onto it, to keep soaring. Persephone had never seen Artemis look as beautiful as she did in that moment. The little blonde splayed herself across the dark-haired goddess, feeling Artemis' climax in the tremble and quiver of the lush, ripe body beneath her own.

"Your turn." Persephone pounced and straddled the red-haired goddess, burying her face into her pink, wet flesh. Athena jumped and squealed in surprise, and Artemis, still panting and shuddering from her own climax, rolled toward them with a smile.

"Our little Sephie is such a fast learner, isn't she?" Artemis cupped the quivering swell of Athena's breast in her hand and their eyes met. Athena smiled, her eyes bright, before turning her attention to the blonde goddess' thighs parted over her head.

Persephone had come to love the taste of them, and more, their response to her probing tongue. Athena gasped and shook underneath her as she accepted Persephone's tongue lapping and poking through her hot, waiting folds. Persephone wiggled over the other goddess' face and rocked when the redhead's mouth found her pearl, sucking and licking like she was going to devour the slender blonde.

Persephone moaned softly, her mouth never leaving the goddess' sweet flesh, as Athena took her ever closer to her peak. She felt herself dangling there, her sex pulsing with a full, throbbing ache. Athena began to use her tongue, centered right over her sensitive omi—a fast, steady rhythm sending Persephone over the edge without a chance of looking back.

"Oh, by the gods!" Persephone cried, feeling a hot, delicious burst of pleasure rocking her body, pressing herself against the other goddess' face, drowning her in juices.

"Mmmmm…" Athena, still slowly lapping, grazed her fingernails over Persephone's wet, blonde curls, parting her wide. "Let's do that again."

Persephone whimpered but locked her mouth back down over Athena's slit, digging in deep with her tongue, greedy to taste more. Out of the corner of her eye, she saw Artemis' hand moving between her own legs and knew the other goddess was pleasuring herself as she watched them. Athena didn't stop licking, her fingers spreading Persephone open, sliding inside of her, pumping in and out. What would it be like with a man? *I want to feel the thick, hot heat of a man inside of me instead.*

Then Athena spread her legs wide, pulling them back to give Persephone even more of her. Persephone took her, probing her fingers deep, twisting and massaging inside, parting the goddess' soft, red curls. Neither of them could talk, their mouths too busy, their tongues lapping. Their muffled cries and moans were like two hungry kittens kneading their mother's belly for milk, wanting more…more…more!

Persephone, gasping and gulping copious amounts of sweetness from Athena's sex, could feel the taut, telltale tremble in the other goddess' thighs that told her how close she was. Persephone couldn't hold back, either, as much as she wanted it to go on forever. The exquisite torture had to end. And it did, exploding between them like a dam breaking, their bodies bucking together as they moaned and shuddered with it.

Turning, Persephone wiggled around and found Athena's mouth and they kissed, their faces full of each other's sweetness. Artemis, licking the wetness of her second climax off her fingers, leaned in to taste, her lips sliding across their wet cheeks. They all giggled together, hugging and rocking in the buzz of the late afternoon.

"So, did that get your mind off things, precious?" Artemis teased, touching a fingertip to the tip of Persephone's nose.

"I suppose." The blonde goddess sighed and stared up at the blue expanse of the sky.

Athena shook her red head, smiling indulgently. "I think our little Sephie needs something extra today."

"Oh?" Artemis raised an eyebrow in the other goddess' direction as she rolled over to lean on her elbow on the other side of Persephone. "What did you have in mind?"

Athena half-sat and began searching through the folds of her robe. "I borrowed something from Aphrodite last night. You know how hard she is to please."

Artemis snorted. "Zeus himself couldn't please that one—even on a good day." She sat up, eager, as Persephone looked between them, wide-eyed. "What is it?"

"Ah, here it is!" Athena slipped a golden phallus-shaped object out of her robes, holding it up in triumph. "Her husband, Hephaestus, made it for her."

"The metal worker?" Persephone stared at the object in Athena's hand as it glinted in the sun. The necklace at her throat had been made by the same man, and Persephone was a little afraid of the power in both objects.

"Yes." Athena smiled, rubbing her hand up and down the length of it. "The magical metal worker. Want to see what it does, my precious Sephie?"

There was no question Persephone did, her curious eyes watching as Athena slid it down between the blonde's legs, rubbing the tip through her slit.

"Ohhh!" Persephone moaned as the phallus slipped inside of her. *Is this what a flesh-and-blood man will feel like?* Her face flushed with the memory of the man in the woods, his hand pumping the length of his erection until it exploded. Artemis propped herself up on her elbow, looking down as the golden shaft disappeared and reappeared, slick with the girl's juices.

"It gets better, darling," Athena assured her, tapping lightly at the end of the phallus.

A gentle hum, like the bees landing on the wildflowers, came from between Persephone's legs, and the blonde felt a vibration deep inside of her. *Certainly a real man's member can't do this!* She moaned, rocking against Athena as the phallus pressed in deeper, harder.

"Feel good?" Artemis kissed the writhing goddess' cheek. Persephone could only gasp and nod, her eyes half-closing in pleasure as Athena tapped the end of the phallus again, turning the hum to a deep, delicious buzz. "Let me see, Sephie…"

Persephone spread herself, tilting her hips toward the dark-haired goddess' heated gaze as Artemis positioned herself between the blonde's thighs. Artemis' tongue moved over her lower lip as she watched the phallus pressing deep into the slender goddess' flesh.

"Let me try." Artemis took the phallus from Athena's hands, catching the same rhythm as she twisted it in and out of the blonde and leaned her mouth over the girl's sex to suck her flesh between her lips.

"Oh!" Persephone opened her eyes to look down at Artemis in surprise, her eyes dazed with pleasure. Athena shifted her attention to Persephone's thick, pink nipples, rolling one between her finger and thumb, making her jump.

Artemis flicked her tongue at Persephone's omi over and over, the fat, swollen bud with its thick hood, giving in to the pressure of her mouth. Persephone moaned as the phallus slid easily in and out of her slippery wetness. She couldn't stop her response. Her head fell back, her hips moved up, and she gave in completely.

Is this what it's like to be taken by a man? The long golden phallus warmed as it plunged into her flesh, its vibrating thickness unforgiving as it pressed deep inside of her, making her gasp and jump.

When Artemis slid it out of Persephone's swollen slit, she replaced it immediately with two of her fingers, crooking them and rubbing at some magic spot deep inside. Persephone cried out, squirming under the goddesses' attention, Athena's mouth and fingers working her nipples and Artemis focusing on her sex.

"Oh! What—?" Persephone's question was lost as Artemis pressed the head of the humming phallus to her slit, right where those light blonde hairs began to curl, still moving her tongue back and forth there. The sensation was beyond heaven and earth and Persephone bucked under them, looking down past her nipples, red as little cherries now under Athena's attention, to meet Artemis' hungry eyes.

Persephone couldn't help moving her hips against the dark-haired goddess, and she began thrashing as Artemis rubbed deep inside at that spot, that sweet, delicious spot. Persephone was so wet she knew Artemis had a hard time keeping her mouth against her flesh, and juices ran down her chin, wetting Persephone's thighs.

"Oh!" Persephone felt something building inside of her, something different, as Artemis pressed even harder inside, stretching the smooth walls of her sex with her fingers again and again. "Oh wait! I don't…please, I can't—"

And then the world exploded as she shuddered all over with a deeper pleasure than she had ever experienced before. Gasping, Persephone grabbed the goddess' dark head and pressed it against her mound. "Don't stop! Don't stop, oh please, please!"

Artemis didn't stop and Persephone rocked her hips and ground against her face, using the goddess' tongue and the humming vibration of the phallus to take herself to the edge once again. Persephone moaned, shoving her pelvis up and mashing her mound against the goddess' mouth as she climaxed again, panting and arching against them both.

"No, no!" Persephone pushed at Artemis with her hands as she continued to lap gently between her legs. "No more, I can't…"

"We want to wear you out, Sephie," Athena reminded her with a mischievous smile as she slid down between Persephone's legs as well. "Remember? Make you forget all about places you can't go, things you can't have…"

"Please!" Persephone begged, shaking her head. "Just your tongue, then…I can't…"

Artemis complied, sliding the phallus down between her own legs, but kept her tongue between Persephone's spread thighs. The dark-haired goddess moaned softly, her eyes meeting Athena's.

"Let's share." Athena rolled Artemis to her back, and the dark-haired goddess' hands grabbed the wiggling Persephone's hips, taking her over. Persephone squirmed against Artemis' relentless tongue, burying her flushed face into one of the robes spread out on the grass.

Persephone glanced over her shoulder and saw the two of them scissoring together, just as she and Artemis had done earlier. Only this time they rubbed the golden head of the phallus between them. The sounds of their pleasure made Persephone dizzy, and Artemis' tongue pushed her to the point of needing release once again. Her sex was so swollen and slick, throbbing between her thighs, and she rocked her hips again, working toward her pinnacle.

"Yes!" Persephone panted. "Please, please!"

The two goddesses moaned and rocked together with the golden phallus riding between them, buzzing in rhythm as they slid it over their flesh. Persephone groaned, hearing their cries, pushing herself toward her own zenith as Artemis' tongue flicked faster and faster between her swollen lips.

Persephone heard the sound of their mutual peak, felt it in the tight grip of Artemis' hands on her hips, and that send her sailing, too. She quivered and spread, her belly tightening and releasing with her climax as her cries joined theirs across the wide open field.

Rolling to the side, Persephone moaned, her ears ringing faintly. She couldn't even see straight and threw a slender arm over her eyes to block out the sun. The buzz of the phallus disappeared and all that was left was the faint hum of the bees as she floated along the river of pleasure still rippling through her body.

"I think Hephaestus' magic phallus has finally done our Sephie in." Athena's voice came from somewhere above her, and Persephone uncovered her eyes but kept them shaded against the brightness.

"Where are you going?" Persephone asked as they stood, arranging their robes and smoothing their hair. It made her dizzy to look up at them, like twin towers of light rising on either side of her.

"There is a hunt." Artemis sounded a little apologetic. She glanced at Athena, who shrugged a shoulder. "Do you...do you want to join us?"

"No." Persephone wrinkled her nose and sighed, putting her hands behind her head and crossing her ankles prettily. "I guess I'll pick a few more flowers for my mother. She loves the wild roses..." Persephone's voice trailed off, and even she heard the melancholy in it.

"You're such a good girl." Athena winked, picking a daisy and dropping it onto Persephone's bare belly. The blonde goddess sighed and rolled her eyes, picking up the flower and twirling it around in her delicate fingers.

"Maybe that's my problem." Persephone plucked a white petal from the yellow center with a vicious tug. "To be good...not to be good...to be good..." She continued to pull petals off, her eyes dark.

"It doesn't last forever, Sephie, I promise." Artemis nudged Persephone's bare hip with her sandaled toe.

"What doesn't?" Persephone looked up from her flower-rending.

"The yearning," Artemis explained. "Like you have a hole inside you can never possibly fill. Some day you will be like us. Strong and capable and independent." Artemis smiled over at Athena and a secret communication passed between them Persephone felt but couldn't decipher.

"Have fun." Persephone sighed again and closed her eyes.

She heard them laughing together as they walked away. There was nothing like the laughter of a goddess. And usually it warmed her very center, but today it made her shudder. She didn't want to grow up to be like them. She wanted to grow up to be like herself. It was just that she didn't know exactly what that was. Strong and capable and independent—those were the things her mother wanted her to be. But she didn't want to live Athena's or Artemis' life. Did she want to wield a sword, or a bow, or an axe? No. Her power somehow existed in another realm. She just didn't know exactly where that was, or how to get there. It was beyond her, and it ached.

Fingering the necklace her mother had given her, she thought about Demeter's rather unfavorable view of men. *Perhaps Mother is right*, she thought, considering what had happened with Pirithous. She couldn't imagine being touched by the old man. Shuddering, she remembered his hands on her, the horrible taste of his tongue in her mouth. But then she recalled the man she had seen chopping wood and how his body had glistened with the sweat of hard work. A man like the woodsman—his strong muscles, bright smile, and dark eyes—yes, she could picture that quite well.

The necklace was cool to the touch now, and Persephone sat up, reaching for the clasp in back, filled with a sudden fear it wouldn't unlatch. It did, though, and she cupped the chain and locket in her palm. No one believed she could take care of herself. Not her mother, not the other goddesses. *Why should I be under a constant watch? Am I not to be trusted?* Sometimes it felt like her mother's love was going to suffocate her.

Persephone dropped the necklace among the flowers with a sigh and stretched out again. She closed her eyes and drifted toward sleep to the sounds of the bees pollinating the regal irises, the delicate lilies and the compelling narcissus all around her tawny sun-kissed body as she languished in the heat. Helios was in fine form today. His flaming chariot was so far from her the bright light burned like a ball of fire across the sky, and thinking of him, feeling his heat, made her feel flushed and a little breathless.

Still, the warmth on her face and limbs was nothing compared to what burned between her thighs. Even after a whole afternoon of goddess pleasure, she still yearned for more. What's missing? Her sweet honey was thick and copious from the goddesses' ministrations, and she couldn't help spreading her legs wider, letting the cool breeze kiss her nether lips and allowing her fingers to linger in the wetness there. She whimpered, sighed, wiggled and longed for something else, something beyond her comprehension.

A quick whiff of warm air over her cheek startled her, and she found herself staring into the steady eye of the blackest horse she had ever seen. She was so surprised, she didn't think to panic or scream or run. She looked askance at the animal, reaching to pet its dark velvet nose as it moved its head to graze beside her.

"Odd...Noire seems to like you." The voice came from behind her, and she scrambled for her clothing, covering herself and flushing at the mere thought of what this new stranger might have seen.

Still a little disoriented from the heat, she saw the horse had a mate. These horses led another team, all attached to a sleek black chariot that seemed to vibrate where it stood, next to a gaping hole in her field that hadn't been there just moments before. Turning, she looked for the owner, but the chariot appeared empty. Where did the voice come from? She blinked fast when an immortal almost twice her size suddenly appeared as he removed a golden helmet from his head. He towered over her, blotting out the sun.

"Sweet Persephone...or should I call you Sephie, like your girlfriends?" His smile was the brightest thing about him, and it appeared just briefly.

"I...where...who are you? Where did you come from?" Persephone stumbled over her words, pulling her garment close around her slight frame and glancing across the fields. No possibility of rescuing figures in the distance marred the vibrant expanse of wildflowers, just a flood of rainbow color on an already bright palette.

"Hephaestus made the helmet for me." He hooked the strap over the edge of the chariot. "Turns anyone who wears it invisible. It's a useful contraption." He lifted his eyes to hers and she saw a deep, orange glow there that took her breath away. "What's the matter? You don't recognize me, Sephie?" He stepped closer to lift her chin. His hand was enormous, and it occurred to her, he could crush her skull within his fist if he wanted. Puzzled, she jerked her head away from his hold and then took an immediate step back. The horse behind her nickered and stomped at the disruption as she pressed against its flank.

"Hades," she whispered, the realization dawning. Her heart beat like a hummingbird in her breast.

"Yes...hmm...unseemly nickname. Aidoneus, originally, and indeed, preferably. You, bright one, can call me Aidon. Few people do," he admitted. He focused on at her bare shoulders, and his eyes traced the curve of her collarbone showing above the shimmering garb she had hastily drawn around her.

"What are you doing up here?"

"Seem out of place, do I? Yes, well...perhaps." He shrugged, leaning forward as if about to tell her a secret. "I came for you."

"Me?" Persephone's eyes widened and her robes dropped along with her jaw. His eyes followed the slip of her gown down the slope of her breasts.

"So, shall we?" He waved her toward the chariot. "The team isn't used to being up top."

She smiled, confused and bemused, and then laughed.

The light sound startled the horses and Noire reared. Aidon reached past Persephone's head to grab the reins, pressing her between his chest and the horse's flank as he did. Her head didn't reach his shoulder. The black robes he wore smelled a little of burning leaves and, beneath that, another musky, earthy smell she wasn't familiar with. It made her dizzy.

He handed her the reins and winked. "Want to drive?"

"I don't...I don't understand." She said the words and some vague memory of a dream she'd once had surfaced for a moment as she looked into his eyes. She didn't have any more time to recall it, but some part of her remembered this, and knew, somehow had always known, that a man—this man—would be coming for her.

"Tell you what, I'll explain it on the way." He swept her up over his shoulder in one swift motion and stepped onto the chariot. She was a small goddess, used to being tossed about, but she was shocked at how fast it was done.

They sprang into his chariot, the earth yawning open. The last thing she saw of the world above was the golden locket in the grass, blazing a bright, angry blue. *If only I hadn't taken it off!* Persephone tried to scream, but found she had no breath. She clung to his side for fear of falling into the black depths, hiding her face in alarm against his robes.

He shifted around, securing her between the front of the chariot and his formidable bulk. She still couldn't stand to look forward, seeing nothing but darkness in front of them. Instead, she stayed turned toward him, burying her face against him and holding fast with two pale, clenched fists. The horses' hooves ran silent, as if speeding on air, but she knew it was black earth, the deep, rich soil the wildflowers thrived in that they tunneled through. Soon she couldn't resist the temptation to see and turned her face, watching the earth give way to a thick, dark sediment.

She was startled by the sound of hooves on gravel. "Where are we going?" She was sure he couldn't hear her over the sound of the horse's hooves and the whirlwind rushing past their ears.

"Paradise..." His voice was as low and tender as a kiss. "The center of the world." When she felt his lips against her hair, his breath hot over her scalp, her stomach lurched. She had never been this close to a man before—her mother had made sure of that up until now. The thought of what he could do—what he might do, what she couldn't stop him from doing—made her pulse race to match the horses' thunder. Yet, there was a moist tingling under her robes. She flushed at her own response, and Aidon seemed to sense her conflict, pressing his hips forward into the curve of her behind.

His voice filled with pride. "Your new home."

Chapter Two

Persephone didn't know if it was his words or the fact the earth around them seemed to turn to a dull, silvery liquid that made her stomach flip, but she turned her face again to hide her dismay and stayed there until she felt the chariot come to a halt.

"Where are we?" She looked up at him, afraid to turn and see.

"I thought you would feel at home here." Aidon rubbed a piece of her hair between his fingers, lifted it to his lips, closed his eyes and inhaled. The gesture both intrigued and scared her. She turned in his arms and gasped at the sight before her.

"Elysium," she breathed, her hands clutching the chariot in surprise.

"Yes." His voice rumbled through his chest and vibrated down her spine.

Persephone sprang out of the chariot and he didn't stop her when she wandered out into the tall grass. Looking up, she saw no sun, yet it was bright as day. Her delicate hands played along the tops of pussy willows and reached for the sunflowers. She paused, breathing in the scent of wildflowers. The gentle edges of wheat grass blended with the golden groundsel and royal violets, and the field stretched that way as far as she could see. An enormous cottonwood tree stood in the middle of the field and, as she watched the leaves move in the cool breeze, a young couple sprang up from beneath it, chasing each other around the trunk.

"Aidon!" She took a step back, and felt him behind her. "Who are they?"

"They are of the chosen. The joyful."

Persephone watched, transfixed, as the man caught the woman and they tumbled, laughing, back to the ground. "They have no clothes?"

"We have very little use for garments here." He smiled at her surprised expression.

Persephone looked back toward the tree and saw the couple kissing, their bodies pressed together and their limbs entwined. She felt a slow heat rising in her belly as she watched. "What are they doing?"

"Something similar to what you and your friends were doing above." Aidon's hands moved over her gown, baring her shoulders.

Persephone gaped, unable to look away as the man turned the woman and pressed her against the tree, entering her from behind. She had heard of such things, of course. Still, she had never seen anyone do what these two did with such passion and intensity. Her breath came faster, her tongue sneaking out to wet her dry lips.

"Open your eyes." Aidon turned her head in another direction. "They are everywhere."

Persephone saw another couple in the grass, the woman on her hands and knees, the man behind her forcing himself into her flesh. A woman cried out, and Persephone turned her head the other way, seeing a man sitting up in the tall grass and thrusting, his eyes closed, his mouth open. How had she not seen them before? The sounds of lust, soft sighs and moans, exhaled all around her.

"Is it what you expected?" His eyes searched her face.

"No." She shook her head before turning to watch the couple by the tree again. The woman had wrapped her arms around the trunk and was moaning.

He nodded. "The rest will be wholly unfamiliar to you."

Those words made Persephone's heart sink. He led her back to the chariot where the horses grazed, their noses finding the sweetest grass.

"Are you taking me back home to my mother?" She looked up at him with pleading eyes.

He frowned. "No." Grabbing the horses' reins, he pressed her into the chariot with his bulk. Then they hastened again, faster than she could have imagined, around the field on a gravel road that jarred her teeth and made her head buzz.

The light grew dim as they traveled, as if the sun were setting. Yet there was no sun, no telltale rosy glow along the horizon. This was more of a darkening, as if one mourning veil after another was being thrown over the world. Persephone steadied herself when the chariot slowed again and stopped. Aidon gripped her shoulders and spun her about to face him. His eyes darkened as he leaned in to kiss her.

It was a brief assault, his tongue forcing its way between her lips. Persephone struggled against him, her pounding fists useless against his chest, her cries unheard against the crushing weight of his mouth. When he stopped and looked at her, he was breathing hard, his hands clamped around her upper arms. She winced, tasting blood as she licked her lips. His gaze roamed over her. His hands followed his eyes, traveling over her arms and across her breasts to the seam of her robe. A smile broke across his face as his finger grasped the edge of the cloth and began to peel it from her form.

"No!" Persephone peered around, seeing just the stretch of endless, graying fields. She could hear a faint hum, like the buzzing of dark bees, but that was all.

"Sephie, I must." His grip loosened as he slid her shift down her shoulders. "You would blind them in this."

"Blind who?" She clutched at her gown, but it was no use. As easily as it went on, it slipped off, and she stood before him wearing nothing.

"The shades." His gaze caressed her breasts, her belly, lingering at the apex of her thighs. She covered herself with her hands and he smiled, but there was no humor in it.

"Aidon," she pleaded. "I must have something to cover me."

"Perhaps..." His finger traced the line of her hip, the indentation of her waist. "You may blind them as you are, beauty. You glow like no other."

"Please!" she implored, her hands gripping his.

He unhooked the mantle of his own chiton, shrugging his shoulders and sliding it off. Persephone stared. His skin was a deep bronze, his chest thickly muscled, his stomach ridged. He covered her, and she pulled the cloth around her, watching it pool at her feet in waves.

"Better?" he asked.

She nodded, averting her eyes from the small dark loincloth that couldn't hide his arousal. The sight of it made her queasy, her stomach doing little flips.

"We're almost home."

She guessed his smile was probably meant to be reassuring, but it sent a cold stab of fear into her heart. This strange place was not her home. She already longed for the sun, for the feel of rain against her cheeks. Aidon drove the chariot onward and Persephone craned to see her virginal white gown pooled in the darkening field. She was certain she would never see it again.

Aidon lashed the reins and the horses galloped faster, and faster still. Persephone clung to his arm as they neared the edge of the field. It looked as if the land dropped away. She could see nothing but darkness beyond.

"Stop!" she screamed. But he didn't, and they sailed off the edge into nothing.

When she dared to open her eyes again, it was gloomy as night. No stars or moon lit the way. The walls of the cavern ahead glowed deep red, like hot coals, illuminating a winding black river.

She felt Aidon's arm at her back, guiding her off the chariot. Stumbling over the hem of his garment, Persephone lifted armloads of the fabric so she could walk. A hand gripped her arm and she gasped, whirling to face a woman cradling a baby in her arms. The woman begged for something, her voice pleading, but Persephone couldn't catch the words.

Persephone frowned up at Aidon. "I don't understand."

"It's the language of the dead." He removed the woman's hand from Persephone and the woman withdrew, sinking to her knees and wailing, rocking her baby back and forth. "She is asking you for coin to pay the boatman.

There." He nodded to the boat coming toward them across the river.

"Can't you let them go? Aren't you ruler here?" Persephone shrank against Aidon's side as more and more people moved toward them from out of the darkness, holding out their hands and speaking in strange, muted tones.

"I have power in the Underworld, but I am not the only one." Aidon held his hand up against the onslaught. The bodies stopped, jostling amongst themselves, their restless limbs jerking. "No shade crosses Styx without paying."

Persephone allowed him to help her into the boat as shades crowded in around them. A hooded, shadowy figure silently held forth a skeletal palm to each of them as they boarded.

"Your chariot?" She watched as the horses began trotting along beside the river.

"They will go home," Aidon assured her. "I wanted to bring you in this way, so you could see."

"See?" Persephone held tightly to the side of the boat as they began to move. It rocked gently as the hooded figure moved them along with a staff raking the bottom of the river.

"Sit." Aidon pulled her to him, tucking her between his strong, powerful thighs. Persephone sat as straight as she could, her breathing shallow, trying to ignore the tickling of his hot breath over her neck.

The trip across the river was short, and the boatman steadied the skiff with his staff as they stepped off. Persephone gathered the extra material of her borrowed garment once again and eyed the craggy surface before stepping onto it. Aidon kept one hand on her arm as they walked around a rocky wall and started down a steep flight of stairs.

A low growl met them at the bottom of the steps, and Persephone backed up against Aidon, clutching at him and finding only the taut skin of his thigh. A trio of massive black dog heads emerged from the shadows below. Their six eyes darted to Persephone, then beyond to Aidon. In unison, the dogs' lips relaxed to cover the bared teeth. One of the heads issued a welcoming bark as the beast stepped forward to reveal all three of its heads attached to one body.

Persephone inhaled a brief gasp and her hand rushed to cover her mouth. She had heard of Cerberus, the great canine who guarded the gates of Tartarus, but no words could have prepared her for the sight of the monster. Aidon pushed past her, rubbing behind the ears of each head before he turned back to Persephone and extended his hand. "Come."

With a gulp, she placed her tiny hand within his, but she kept her wide eyes glued to the beast until the shadows had again reclaimed its form. Only then did she turn her eyes forward and get her first glimpse of Hell. The cavern walls weren't red, but rather black. The only light was a shimmer coming from the glow of two luminescent silver pools flanking a ghostly white cypress tree.

Persephone clutched at Aidon's elbow. "What is this place?"

"The Chamber of Judgment."

She pointed to the dozens of forms sliding in and out of one of the pools. "And who are they?"

"They are the shades." He put his hand over hers. "That is the Pool of Lethe. It erases all memory."

Persephone pushed her body against his. "But, why?"

Aidon caressed her head, her hair. She watched his face soften, shimmering in the glimmer of the pools. "It is painful for the dead to remember the living."

"What about that one?"

"The Pool of Mnemosyne—Memory."

Persephone looked up at him, her brow furrowed. "Why does no one swim there?"

"It is for the Initiates," he explained. Persephone crossed her arms over her breasts as if cold, even though beads of perspiration had already formed on her forehead. "You will come to understand our ways."

"What if I don't want to?" Tears stung her eyes as she looked upward to him.

Aidon frowned, his eyed darkening. "You will."

She noticed for the first time the ebony throne sitting above the pools, and the three smaller ones off to the left. "And those?"

"Look who's home!"

They both turned at the sound of a feminine voice. Persephone barely stifled a scream as she beheld the woman and the slender black snakes on her head, where her hair should have been, hissing in deadly chorus. Though Persephone did not cry out, she couldn't help stepping behind Aidon.

"Ah, Tisi!" He strode to embrace the woman. "Persephone, I'd like you to meet Tisiphone. She is one of the Erinyes—a Fury."

Persephone extended her hand, a well-mannered gesture, as her eyes took in the form of the nude woman. The Fury stood as tall as Aidon, her skin like dull silver, and her eyes glowed red as she swept them over Persephone.

"My pleasure." Tisi's smile showed sharp, white fangs. "So this is your new bride?"

Persephone started, looking between them. "What?"

Tisi covered her smile with a clawed hand. "Oh goodness, I didn't let the cat out of the bag, did I?"

Aidon glared. "Thanks, Tisi. You can go."

The Fury turned, and Persephone saw great black wings tucked neatly behind her.

"Bride?" Persephone's heart fluttered in her chest.

Aidon sighed, covering the small of her back with his palm. "Let's find you something else to wear."

"Bride?" she repeated, her mouth barely working, her trembling hand hovering near her throat. She had a sudden flash of memory—her mother's gentle kiss just this morning and her accompanying admonishment to be careful.

She whirled on him, her face drained of blood. "No! You can't mean to keep me here!"

Aidon's mouth opened but no words came out. He just nodded.

"No!" She clawed at his chest, biting at him, snarling.

He wrapped both of her wrists in one of his hands and let her rail until she collapsed against him. "Why did you think I brought you down here?" Her pain drew the attention of the shades, and they stood transfixed, watching them.

Persephone shook her head. Until this moment, she had been seduced by the mystery and strangeness of it all, but the thought of staying here forever sent her reeling. She turned away from him and vomited, retching over and over. Aidon held her racking body until her heaves subsided. When she wiped her mouth with the back of her hand and looked up at him, his eyes grew dark, his mouth set in a grim line. "You are mine."

She turned to face him, her knees shaking every bit as much as her voice. "I belong to no one."

He smiled. "Oh, but you do."

Persephone's eyes narrowed as she shed the burden of the heavy robe. "Memories can be unbearable for the living, too." With that, she turned and raced across the rocky surface toward the Pool of Lethe.

* * * *

Consciousness returned slowly to Persephone. The bed beneath her was firm but not uncomfortable. Shaking her head to clear the fuzz, she moved to sit and found her wrists shackled above her head. She felt a strain under her arms, in her ribs.

How long have I been like this? She opened her mouth to speak, but her lips felt so dry she could barely part them.

She managed a low moan as a strange, yet familiar face bent over her. It was a dark figure, his cheeks gaunt and pale, his mouth red and smiling. She had dreamed about him. His eyes reflected like large, violet pools, and she found herself transfixed in them. Her breath slowed, her heart's murmur tamed to an easy, steady beat. He lifted a bottle full of tiny luminous crystals, like glowing sand, and began to open it.

"No, Hypnos." Aidon's voice came out of the darkness. "No more. Leave us."

The figure frowned but stepped back into the shadows and was gone. Persephone strained to see Aidon, noticing her wrists bound but her ankles free. She recalled everything—her abduction, her trip into the Underworld, her desperate run toward the Pool of Lethe to purge herself of her memory. Yet she still remembered...

"Please." Her voice was a thick croak. "Release me."

He came out of the darkness to stand beside the huge bed. "How is your head?" His fingers rubbed through her hair and she winced when he caressed a knot there that throbbed dully with her pulse under his touch.

"What happened?"

He frowned. "You fell before you reached the Pool of Lethe. Your memory is intact, although you've got quite a bump there. I had Hypnos give you his pain-sleep until you were healed."

"How long have I been here?"

His fingers trailed down her cheek. "A day...no more."

"Please, I'm begging you. Take me home to my mother." She implored him with her eyes, but he didn't see her pleading orbs as his gaze swept over her body, uncovered against the black velvet bedclothes.

"Do you know what you look like, lying here?" His finger traced the velvet around her body, not touching her skin. She shook her head, feeling her hair brush her cheeks with the motion.

"The brightest jewel in my kingdom." His smile was determined, almost cruel. She shivered as he continued, "Did you know I own all of the riches below the earth? All the gold, the silver, the diamonds...they all belong to the ruler of the Underworld."

She shook her head again, not trusting her voice. He knelt beside her and she saw he was naked. Swallowing hard, she looked up to his face. "You shine brighter than any diamond. I had to have you, Sephie."

Persephone closed her eyes, shaking her head and feeling tears slip down her temples. Shocked by the weight of him next to her on the bed, she stiffened. His palm stroked the skin of her belly, neutral ground between two sensitive poles. The warmth of his hand was like a brand, setting her skin afire.

Persephone sought to distract him and perhaps delay the inevitable. "Water. Please, Aidon." He reached out and retrieved a chalice, lifting it to her lips. She drank greedily, the liquid spilling down her chin.

"Easy, now…" His eyes lingered over the droplets on her throat.

She tilted her head, indicating she'd had enough. "Thank you."

"Now, try this." He reached for a second chalice, this one containing an amber liquid, and held it to her lips. She took a hesitant sip, then closed her mouth and turned away. The liquid burned her throat. She made a face, coughing.

"It's an acquired taste." He chuckled.

Her thirst abated, she felt warm, though her head felt a little fuzzy again. "Can you untie me?"

"I don't think so." He shook his head, his admiring gaze running up the slope of her arms raised above her head. "Only a falconer knows when it's time to untether the falcon."

She looked at him, tears brimming. "Where can I go? I'm in Hell."

Aidon frowned and then sighed. He reached above her head and untied her arms. She groaned, rubbing her flesh to let a little feeling back. They tingled and throbbed as they came back to life.

"Thank you."

Aidon lifted her hand, kissing the marks on her wrists from the binding. Persephone watched him, his tongue flicking the inside of her wrist, making her shiver. Her skin was as soft and delicate as papyrus and she bruised very easily. Their eyes locked and his glowed a deep, warm amber in the darkness, something she hadn't noticed before.

"It hurts..." She rubbed at her wrist. His hands swallowed her forearm as he massaged her. He bent to kiss the inside of her arm up to her elbow. Persephone's breath came faster as she observed him. He pressed himself against her, tracing her mouth with his finger, his eyes following the line of her lips.

He kissed her lightly, licking the corner of her mouth. "You taste like liquid sunshine."

She giggled and blushed. He kissed her again, his tongue pressing between her lips, tasting her more deeply. Persephone pushed against his chest with her hands, fighting his passion, but it was a useless gesture. He slid his leg over hers, the weight of him crushing her.

"No!" She turned her head and gasped for breath, twisting beneath him. Her refusal made him rougher and he took her wrists in his hand, lifting them above her head as he sucked at the tender flesh of her throat. She felt the hard heat of his manhood against the soft flesh of her thigh and she shuddered, struggling for her freedom.

She willed herself to hold still while he tongued his way to her breasts. His mouth covered her delicate pink nipple, sucking hard. She arched her back, moaning, and she felt him smile. He let her wrists go so he could fill his hands with her breasts, kneading them, pressing them together.

Persephone held her breath, her eyes scanning the perimeter of the darkened room, looking for the hint of a door. She glimpsed a large bowl brimming with fruit on a table next to the bed.

His tongue traced circles down her belly and she opened her legs for him. He looked up at her in wonder, and she smiled. Grabbing her hips, he breathed in the scent of her before leaning in to taste the sweet nectar flowing between her legs. Persephone whimpered, ignoring the thought that she didn't want this. With his tongue moving there, she forgot everything. When his finger found the entrance to her heaven, she remembered, and found her strength.

Persephone's legs had all her leverage and she used them, planting her heels against his shoulders and pushing hard. She didn't succeed in moving him, but her body launched upwards on the bed. Rolling to the side, she bolted in the direction Hypnos had disappeared. She heard him behind her as the handle slid in her hand. Locked! She turned, breathless, frantically searching for another exit. Then Aidon was upon her, his eyes blazing the color of fire.

He caught her arm, twisting it behind her and pressing her hard against the door. "Don't move!"

"No!" She screamed.

His mouth moved against her hair as his body crushed her with the weight of the world. "I am very patient, Persephone, but you have just pushed me past my limit!"

"I'm sorry!" Her voice was a reedy hiss, but she sensed it was too late. He grabbed the back of her head, pulling her by her hair. She screamed again, this time in pain and shock. He used his body as a restraining device, flattening her belly against a cold slab of wall.

"What have I offered you that is so awful?" He reached for a restraint shackled to the wall, lifted her wrist and clicked the lock into place. "Why would you want to leave me?" Persephone began struggling harder, but the angry thrust of him against her sent the air from her lungs. "There are fields to play in here." He grabbed her other wrist. CLICK. The sound of the second restraint closed her eyes in resignation.

Aidon's breath was labored now as he pulled her legs apart, reaching for the manacles attached to the wall near the floor. "There are wonders here, Persephone. Riches beyond imagination. I am offering them to you." CLICK. One leg was secure.

Persephone looked up at the chains holding her. Thick and heavy, they allowed her enough leeway to bring her hands together above her head, but that was all.

CLICK. "Am I so hideous?" Aidon looked up at her, one knee on the floor at the last restraining point.

She glanced over her shoulder at him. The look on his face was pained. Standing, Aidon ran a hand down her back and the golden cascade of her hair. His touch was firm, but not rough. He cupped the globe of her bottom and tightly squeezed. "You are mine, Persephone."

Pressing her forehead to the wall, she closed her eyes and whispered, "No." She heard him moving around the room, and endeavored to see, but couldn't.

Aidon's voice came from the other end of the room. "The furies have these things…called scourges. Do you know what they are?" She heard cupboards or drawers being opened and closed. He went on as if she had responded to him. "They're whips, made of dozens of leather strips, with a brass tip on each end." His voice grew more immediate. "Tisi…she has a scourge with scorpions on each tip." Her heart raced, her mouth turning dry. The world felt like it tilted sideways. She pulled hard on the manacles, but there was no give. "Creative girl, that one." His voice was right behind her now, but she couldn't turn her head far enough in either direction to see him.

Persephone moaned, and pleaded with him. "Please, don't. Whatever it is you're thinking of doing, Aidon, please—" She jumped when she felt soft, leather tendrils trailing over her shoulder.

"This isn't a scourge." He traced the thick, heavy straps over her back and bottom. "Just a cat o'nine tails. It won't tear the flesh from you."

Persephone's whole body trembled, her mind reeling. "Aidon, no, please—"

"But when I am through…" Aidon slid his hand under the weight of her hair, slipping it over her shoulder to expose her back and bottom completely. "You will be saying yes."

"No!" She willed herself not to scream. There seemed no use. Still, the first strike across her bare back shocked her. She whimpered, moving as far as the chains would allow away from the source of the blow. Two more quick smacks to her bottom followed, stinging her flesh. Tears sprung to her eyes.

"You are mine, Persephone." Aidon's voice attempted to soothe or seduce, she wasn't sure which. She clung to it in the darkness.

"No!" Another crack of the whip needled her upper thighs. She writhed, straining against the manacles, twisting her wrists, hoping her slight frame and the fine sheen of sweat over her body might allow her to slip out of them. It was no use.

"Yes, bright one." His voice sounded like darkness itself. Another blow fell, this one wrapping around her hip, finding new territory to burn. She bit her lip to keep from screaming and tasted her own blood. The next three strokes from the whip wrenched another hoarse "No!" from her throat.

Aidon's breath came in labored bursts, as if beating her was quite a chore. "Yes, love. You will be my queen." His hand moved over her bottom and Persephone gasped at the sensation, the caress cooling the heat of her raw flesh. It was heavenly and she sighed, arching her back. Her mind screamed no, but her body responded in spite of her inner protests. Her bottom burned and the cool caress of his hand was welcome respite. She recognized the familiar, swelling pulse between her thighs and the tell-tale wetness.

"Yes." He slipped his hand down one of her thighs, opening them. "Say yes."

She shook her head, squeezing her eyes shut against it, and managed another strangled, "No!" *I'm Persephone, the Goddess of Spring, the daughter of Demeter! I'm not meant for this humiliation, this degradation!*

Aidon sighed, backing away from her again. Her whole body stiffened in anticipation. The lashes began, landing again and again on the soft, rounded flesh of her behind until she felt her cheeks on fire. Every stroke broke down her defenses, stripping away the façade. The good girl she was supposed to be, the sweet, innocent maiden, was melting in the heat of her beating.

She willed herself not to scream, and she managed, biting the inside of her cheek and whimpering. She lost count of the blows. She lost track of the time. She lost sight of anything but the darkness behind her eyes. She lost herself. She was no longer her mother's daughter—Persephone the Virgin Goddess of Spring—she was more than that and nothing all at once.

The feel of the whip sent the harsh realization through her body in a way that nothing else ever had. The sting turned to a bright red heat, and her skin tingled with new life as Aidon brought the cat o'nine tails down across her pale flesh. Something was happening. Her body was responding, and she had no control over it. She began to writhe under the leather straps, and every blow made her squirm and arch back for more.

She finally understood the longing for freedom she had felt. She had never known anything like this. Athena and Artemis and even her mother, Demeter, had found their versions in their own strong, capable independence. But Persephone had always felt something lacking in it. Now it was clear.

She didn't want to belong to her mother, or even to herself. She wanted to belong to a man—to be tamed, taken, and forced to surrender. Her freedom was in every harsh caress, the breaking down of everything she believed she was, until she was finally stripped bare and defenseless. It was only when this realization came to her, when it seeped through the cracks in her outer veneer like water trickling in through the bursting seams of a dam, that Aidon ceased.

Just when she thought he would never stop, that the world would go on this way in a red, thrashing haze forever, the clatter of the wooden handle upon the black stone floor reached her ears. Somehow he must have known, have sensed her epiphany. Dazed and panting, she pressed her hot, tear-stained cheek to the wall. The glow of her cheeks and her behind matched the heat between her legs. There was a thick pulse beating there, an ache that demanded attention.

"Sephie." His breath moved coolness over the flushed skin of her neck. "Say yes."

Persephone lowered her head, breathing hard, swallowing past the lump in her throat. She was helpless. Strung up by him. Whipped by him. At his mercy. There was nothing she could do to stop this. Nothing. The certainty shuddered through her and made the steady throb at her core even stronger.

Aidon slipped his hand down her back, over the searing flesh of her bottom, and his fingers eased between her legs, probing there. Her wetness was a betrayal, flowing beyond her borders and onto her thighs. "You're enjoying this, aren't you?" He brought his fingers to his lips, sucking at her juices. He leaned in to capture her mouth. "Tell me. The truth."

Persephone shook her head, pursing her lips against his kiss, denying it. Aidon's hand caressed the hot, reddened skin of her behind, making her shiver. He gave her a wicked smile and then brought his hand down hard, smacking her soundly. She gasped, startled at the sensation.

"I had sought to punish you," he murmured, trailing his fingers down the side of her hip. "But it seems this pain pleases you." Again his hand met the soft skin of her behind with a resounding slap and Persephone jumped, hissing air through her teeth. "There is often a fine line, between pleasure and pain, life and death. Did you know that, little one?" Persephone shook her head and moaned as his hand struck again, the reverberation rumbling her whole pelvis.

"It is an art, this pleasure-making from pain." His hand lost itself in her hair and then he pulled, jerking her head back so his mouth pressed to her ear. She swallowed hard, feeling his big body pushing against hers. The cold, black obsidian bit her flesh as he used his mass to keep her there, his hand still clenched into a fist in her hair. "Not many know how to do so, and many more do not care for it."

His knee parted her thighs from behind, forcing her to spread her legs. Persephone gasped, trembling under him. He kissed her hard, his lips bruising, his tongue invading. She moaned, her body arching into his as she kissed him back, twisting in his grip and finding she could not resist him.

When the kiss ended, his eyes glowed in the dimness, and he had a small, satisfied smile on his face. "You like the struggle, don't you?" He leaned into her small form until she could barely breathe, crushing her. She squirmed underneath him. The more she twisted, the tighter he held her. Persephone finally gave up, breathless and flushed, the heat between her legs resting solidly against his thigh like a hot pulse. His excitement at her distress was apparent. She felt his thick length pressed like a steel rod against her behind.

"Oh, Sephie," he murmured, raining kisses over her flushed face. "I knew the moment I set eyes on you I had to have you...and now I know why."

"No!" she gasped, twisting in his arms, resuming the battle. He let her, his strength more than enough to keep her as she squirmed and strained against him. Panting, she moaned as he slipped a hand between her thighs, the incredible heat nothing compared to the slick wetness there. He cupped her whole mound and lifted her high up off the ground, pulling the chains around her ankles to their maximum length.

Persephone gasped, panicking, as her body slid upwards along the cold wall, the edges of the stone biting into her soft flesh. Aidon held her there, cupping her sex and using his weight to keep her dangling, like a helpless doll. The feeling was a relief and she melted into the sensation. There was no rubbing or massaging. He just held her there and waited, as if he could stay there forever.

"You want this." Aidon's breath tickled her ear. "I can feel your body responding to me."

"Please…" She closed her eyes against it, wanting to deny what he said was true. "Please don't do this."

"Ah, but I do believe you want me to do this." His voice rumbled through his chest, and she felt it through her whole body as he spoke. When he rocked her gently back and forth, shifting her weight with just his palm, she couldn't help moaning softly. Slowly, he eased her to the floor. When he moved his bulk away from her, she glanced back over her shoulder. "Your mouth and your body are speaking two different tongues."

"I don't—" Her words were stopped by his hand, pressed firmly over her mouth.

"No more talking." He bore down against her lower back, leaning her forward. "The only word I want to hear from you is 'yes.' Now bend over."

He pulled her feet out as far as the chains would allow and pressed her cheek against the wall. Her arms dangled above her head and it was an awkward position, forcing her bottom out, exposing it to him.

"I have whips and crops and all sorts of delightful implements for us to explore." He caressed her behind, moving his palm over the soft skin. He parted her thighs with his big hands, spreading her legs wide. "And we will, sweetness. Believe me, we will." She gasped when his hand came down on her bottom. "I will be the instrument of your greatest pain and pleasure." The sound of his palm biting her flesh made a resounding slap and she bit her lip, trying not to cry out. "I will be your sun…your moon…" He punctuated each word with a hard swat. "Your day…your night…" Persephone felt the impact vibrating through her. "Your heaven…your hell…"

He had found a rhythm. His palm connected solidly with her bottom, and his fingers grazed her sex with every pass. With each blow, something in her coiled, stretching a little tighter, and waited to spring. Persephone moaned and squirmed, struggling against her restraints, unable to break free from this exquisite torture. The skin of her bottom sang in pain, but the throb between her legs grew wildly as he spanked her.

"And you will be my queen..." His breath came as fast as hers, his hand working in short, hard bursts against her flesh, again and again. She knew what was coming, and she braced herself for it, unable to refuse her body's release. His hand turned and slapped hard and fast at her sex as he leaned into her. Persephone moaned and shuddered with her climax, bucking up against the delicious bite of his hand. His panting breath in her ear was hot and made her shiver. "And you will bow only to me in service and utter surrender."

Persephone closed her eyes. Her skin was on fire, but the undeniable heat at the apex of her thighs was beyond anything she had ever known. Behind her closed eyes, she floated above the world. Bound and beaten, her flesh burning and alive, she felt more free than she ever had in her life. She had longed for something more, had been aching and yearning for something greater than herself. And now she knew she had found it.

"You were meant to be mine." His hand caressed her now, massaging. She sighed and arched against his touch. "Say yes, Persephone."

She had already given herself to him. She felt it in the sinking of her body and flight of her soul. A cage had opened in her heart and something had been set free. His breath over her skin was like the touch of wings and she turned her head to look at him, her eyes soft. He looked at her as if she was already a queen, and she realized she was. "Yes." It was the word they both knew she would say.

He caressed her cheek, wiping her tears with his thumb. "Yes," he repeated, smiling. He unshackled her, and she fell to her knees while he undid her ankle restraints. Standing, he placed a hand on top of her golden head. "Look at me."

She lifted her chin, still feeling the weight of his hand, looking up the length of his arm and into his eyes.

"You are free, Persephone." He removed his hand, letting it drop to his side. "You may go if you wish."

Aidon stepped back and watched her. With her hand on the wall behind her, Persephone tried out her trembling legs. They were steady enough to allow her to rise. She glanced at the door and back at him. *He's letting me go?* She thought of her mother, who must be worried sick, and she took two steps toward liberty.

Then she twisted to look at him, her heart beating hard, like a heavy weight in her chest, and remembered the other kind of freedom she had experienced—the kind of freedom he offered. Torn, she stood, hesitating. He made no move to stop her. She took another step toward the door, and another. Her hand touched the knob, turned it, and she found it unlocked. Glancing behind her, she saw him standing motionless, waiting.

She saw her life, stretched out before her. Endless hours of springtime, romps in the wildflowers with the other goddesses, her mother's protection and care. Yet none of it compared to the feelings Aidon had stirred in her. He looked at her as if he wanted her, as if he could swallow her whole, consume her and make her his in one bite.

She tried to imagine her life here, in the Underworld, and found she could not. There were no familiar images. There was no frame of reference—just Aidon, with his large hands guiding her and his eyes following her.

Closing the door, she turned back to face him. Her bare feet made no sound on the cold onyx floor, and she stopped when she drew close enough that her breath moved the hairs on his chest. Slowly, she knelt, bowing her head, resting her hands on her knees.

"Yes." Her voice didn't waver. She felt his hand on the top of her head and she looked up into his moist eyes. Something passed between them. She didn't understand it, but she felt it, like a hot electric current singing in her belly. "I will stay."

"Do you understand what that means?" His fingers moved down her cheek, tilting her chin up. She opened her mouth to respond, but instead just shook her head, swallowing hard. He rubbed his thumb over her lips, his eyes growing dark with lust. "You don't know...but you will." He reached down to scoop her off the floor and carry her to the velvet darkness of his bed.

Chapter Three

He claimed her with his kiss. Her mouth didn't feel like her own when she opened for his tongue. The probing flesh sent sparks through her body on an intricate web, moving from her center to her very edges and back again. The sensation overwhelmed her and her fingers tangled in his dark hair as she slanted her mouth across his, sucking at his tongue. He moaned, grabbing her wrists and pressing them above her head, leaving her helpless to his lips, his weight. As he pressed himself between her thighs and she felt the steel heat of him, it stayed firm between them, a pulsing petition for entry.

"Can't breathe," she gasped as the kiss broke. He smiled an apology as he knelt up. His glowing eyes swept over her form, searing a trail from the flaxen hair on her head to the sweet, caramel-colored thicket below. He still held both crossed wrists clasped in one hand, but with his other, his fingers brushed over her mound, leaning in and pressing up against her so she felt the insistence of his erection sliding along her crevice.

Holding her wrists up, Aidon leaned in and sucked at her nipples. He flicked them with his tongue and they hardened like smooth, pink pebbles between his lips. Persephone sighed and moaned, wrapping her legs around him and writhing, nudging the tip of him between her swollen lips.

When she struggled in his grasp, trying to free her hands, she was unable. His grip tightened like a vise and she found her breath gone again. He nuzzled her neck, feathering kisses there, nosing around her ear, licking her earlobe. The sensations shot electric sparks down her spine and straight to her pelvis, which seemed to be rocking against him all on its own. She simply couldn't control it.

"Please—" Persephone's words met his mouth as he tried to devour her. The intensity of his kiss flooded her head with a dizzy heat. His tongue left scorching trails of wetness over her breasts and down her belly. She twisted her wrists in his grip, whimpering as he dipped his tongue into her navel. Giving in to him, to this, was nothing like she had imagined it would be. "Please let me go!"

"Never." He sat up, his erection blazing like a towering inferno up against her thigh. She looked at it and then up at him, her eyes wide. "You're mine now." His words and his weight crushed her as he captured her mouth again. It was a hard kiss, and he sucked her tongue deep into his mouth before biting gently at her lips, her chin, her cheek.

"No!" Persephone struggled and kicked as he straddled her ribcage, holding his throbbing length in one hand. He teased the wet head over her nipples as she squirmed and moaned under him, thrashing on the bed. He seemed to enjoy her struggle.

"You keep saying that..." Aidon moved up closer, easing the tip of his erection toward her mouth, still grasping her wrists and holding them high above her head. "Maybe we should give that little mouth something else to do?"

Persephone didn't know what she was doing. Going on instinct alone as he slid the thick length between her tender lips, she began to suck. She had never seen one so close up, let alone had one in her hand or mouth—or anywhere else for that matter. His deep growls and thrusting frightened her at first, but the look of pleasure on his face won her over. He grew harder, his eyes closing as his hips began to drive forward. He clearly forgot about her wrists, letting them go as she sucked him like a hungry, greedy, nursing baby. Her hands went to his thighs, rubbing her soft palms over the thick muscles there. He groaned, losing his hand in her hair and pressing himself deeper into her throat.

Gagging, she pushed against him, trying to turn. He eased back, petting her head before sliding down and kneeling between her legs again. The sight of him rising above her, the strength and heat of him, both frightened and excited her. She had imagined this moment a million times, but the reality of a man was far from her hazy, soft-focus fantasy. His eyes darkened with lust and purpose as he pressed the head of his erection into her mouth.

Panicked, Persephone reached for him, grabbing his length and squeezing. He groaned and thrust into her hand. His fingers probed her sex, parting her and finding her slippery, virgin orifice. One finger slid in easily, but she gasped and squeezed him hard when he slipped in two, then three. His thumb pressed the sensitive spot at the top of her cleft, rubbing there as he moved his fingers slowly in and out.

She rocked her hips back against his hand, delighting in the sensation, but then, a vision of her mother appeared in the darkness behind her closed eyes. Men only want one thing. Persephone knew it was true. She knew what he wanted, what this was leading up to. If she let him take her now, everything was lost. She would no longer be her mother's daughter, the "innocent flower," a "tender bud of spring."

Her eyes flew open, but it was too late. Aidon's weight crushed her again as he removed his hand and slid the swollen tip along her crevice, all the way to the top. She gasped, struggling under him as he rocked his hips, easing the head back and forth over the hot jewel of flesh there.

"No!" she begged, her panicked eyes meeting his. "Please, don't do this!"

His eyes told her he was determined to keep going, to press on, to take her, make her his. Her virgin body trembled while her mind screamed and she tried to fight him. Her hands pressed against his chest, her torso twisting under his. Without a word, he grabbed her wrists again, using one hand to hold them above her head.

"Persephone." The sound of her name on his lips made her pause. "Look at me."

She shook her head. She didn't want to. Her eyes clenched tight, and her hands balled into fists. The aching throb between her legs continued, unabated, and she tried to ignore it as Aidon rocked gently, moving his length up and down her slit.

"Let your body tell you what it wants," he urged, whispering the words into her ear as he pressed her thighs open with his. His hips rolled like thunder, using his thick, hot length where their bodies touched in the wetness, making a delicious friction that built up as he rubbed her, again and again. "I want you to tell me, Sephie."

"No," she whispered, her eyes fluttering open and then closed again. But he was right—her body knew what it wanted. Her legs opened wider, and that feeling, like a ripe, exquisite fruit grown full to bursting, spread through her belly. Her hips began to dance on their own underneath him, around and around the ridged edges of him. "Oh please, don't…oh please…"

"Tell me." He moved like lightning, the wet sound of their flesh rubbing together filling the room. "Don't be afraid. Tell me."

"No!" Her hips bucked up to meet him, the feeling in her loins a tight, throbbing ache. Her body gave in, and she was giving in too. "Ohhhh nooo…"

"Yes!" He urged, his breath coming as fast as hers. She met his eyes in the dimness, hers half-closed and glazed with her coming climax. "Tell me!"

Her whole body trembled with the word. "Yes!" The pulsing wave of her fleshy pink rosebud opened and flooded him with a sticky, girlish honey. "Yes, ohhhh yes. Yes!" She shuddered against him, her thighs quivering. He probed the sensitive, tender folds of flesh, seeking entry. Still reeling, her assent still pouting on her lips, she took his weight as he pressed her thighs wider with his own. The heat of him was like an iron bar pressing into her flesh.

"Ohhh, no!" she cried, her nails digging into his back as he eased into her.

"Yes!" He groaned, forging his way into her depths. Persephone bit back a scream, clutching him tightly and burying her face into his neck. He stopped, his lips grazing her hairline. "You are mine."

His hips ground slowly against her, rocking. She moaned, feeling a sob rise to her throat. She felt him inside of her, at her very core, penetrating the deepest part of her. There was no going back, now. She was his.

"Aidon." She sought the gleam of his eyes in the dimness. He stopped for a moment, lost in her gaze, the thick pulse between them continuing to throb. She struggled against his grasp, twisting her wrists. "Let me go. Please." He did, his body tensing and then slowly relaxing as she touched his cheek, running her hand through his hair.

"Persephone!" He groaned when she slipped her hand down to touch the slick, wet place where their bodies met.

"Yes, Aidon." She had been afraid to speak the words, afraid to make it real, but she wasn't afraid anymore. Lifting her hips up slightly, she wrapped her legs around him. "Yes!"

Her words drove him into her, again and again. She clung to him and allowed herself to be taken, listening to the sweet, slippery music they made as they coupled. She breathed their scent, like black licorice root and roses. She had never felt so free.

His thrusts came harder, faster, deeper. Persephone nibbled his neck, the gentle grind becoming a delightful, persistent, rising hum. She made easy circles with her little hips, dancing against him, and he growled.

Her whole body began to quake beneath him with her pleasure. His body stiffened at the flutter and pulse of her, pushing himself deep and spilling his seed into her belly in hot, fiery bursts. Persephone felt it seeping like lava down her thighs. She stared into the darkness beyond them both as he rolled beside her. In her chest, her heart beat the chorus of his name and she had never felt more at home. She turned to him, pressing her belly to his, the wetness of their flesh a cool reminder.

He touched his forehead to hers, his eyes smoldering in the dimness. She tried to make sense of what her body seemed to want as their breathing slowly returned to normal. She had often fantasized about the man she would give her innocence to, the man she would fall in love with and marry, but never in her wildest dreams had she imagined this. She didn't love him, but he had taken her, possessed her, and somehow made her his.

* * * *

"This better be important!" Aidon yelled as he yanked the door open.

A beautiful goddess with black hair hanging almost to her knees carried a torch into the room. She smiled brightly and cocked her head at him. Persephone pulled the dark sheet around her nakedness, watching from the bed as the young goddess' gaze traveled down the length of Aidon's body and back up again. Persephone frowned, seeing the goddess' eyes linger between his legs.

Aidon sighed. "Hecate, I'm busy—if you hadn't noticed. What is it?"

Hecate's dark eyes flickered over to the bed, where Persephone tried to make herself as small as possible. "Your new bride? Tisi mentioned something—the Goddess of Spring? She's so young! Aidon, are you trying to recapture your youth with nubile young virgins? What's next, a new red chariot?"

She called him Aidon! Persephone crept a little closer, edging along the mattress, so she could hear them better. *Who is this Hecate to him?* She remembered his words. *You can call me Aidon—few people do.*

Aidon snorted. "Did you come here to catch up on Underworld gossip? Because unless there's a problem—"

"As a matter of fact, there is." Hecate raised her delicately arched eyebrow at him. "Unless you've abdicated your responsibilities as God of the Underworld, now that you're engaged?"

Persephone saw Aidon's jaw working as he glared at the dark-haired goddess. "What is it, Hecate?"

"Look, I'm just trying to help you out and stave off some of Tisi's bloodlust..." Hecate moved into the room, sweeping past Aidon, and Persephone noticed for the first time that, like Tisi, the goddess was completely nude. Hecate's body was full and lush, her breasts like ripe fruit, her legs long and shapely as she advanced toward the bed. "But if you'd rather ignore your kingdom for...my, she is a bright little thing, isn't she?" Hecate peered over the dark bed rail, holding her torch up so she could see better, her eyes moving down over the crown of Persephone's golden head. The blonde goddess shrank back from the flame, pulling the sheet up to her neck. "Oh, don't worry, precious, this fire can't burn you. Go ahead, touch it."

Persephone's eyes widened and she glanced over at Aidon. He winked and nodded as Hecate tilted the fiery light toward their bed. Persephone should have felt a great heat from the torch, but there seemed to be nothing emanating from the flame but illumination. Tentatively, she reached her hand out, easing it toward the fire.

Hecate smiled as she waved the torch past Persephone's hesitating hand, passing the flame through her fingers. Acting out of instinct, Persephone jerked her hand back and stared at her skin in disbelief. There was no burn, and she had felt no heat!

The dark-haired goddess winked, looking delighted at her trick. "I told you."

"Our Hecate is full of surprises." Aidon held his hand out toward Persephone, indicating she should come to him. "Sephie, I'm afraid I have some work to do." He smiled at the dark-haired goddess. "Hecate, perhaps you might take my young bride on a tour? Show her the Underworld...and the rest of your enchanting ways?"

Hecate's eyes brightened at his words as she looked between them for a moment, and then she smiled at Persephone. "Sure, I'd be happy to."

"Come, Persephone." Aidon's command was clear as he pulled on and tied his loincloth.

"My clothing…" Persephone searched the room with her eyes, glancing again at Hecate's nude form.

Shaking his head, Aidon's hot gaze swept over her. "You will wear nothing here. That is the way I wish it."

Until today, she had only ever been nude in the presence of the other goddesses or her mother, and the thought of walking naked amongst the things that might lurk in the Underworld made her shiver. Her eyes searched his, as if to ask if his request was sincere, but his look left no room for doubt. Standing, Persephone took his hand, swallowing past her twinge of shame and humiliation.

"You'll get used to it." Hecate leaned in to whisper the words to Persephone as she passed.

"She will come to understand our ways." Aidon's hand pressed Persephone's as they walked toward the door. He looked pointedly over his shoulder at Hecate. "And I know you'll do everything you can to make her comfortable. Right, Hecate?"

The dark-haired goddess took Persephone's other hand and squeezed it. She couldn't tell if Hecate's smile was sincere or not, but the other goddess winked at her and said, "Of course. I think we can have lots of fun."

Aidon raised his eyebrows. "Not too much fun."

Hecate laughed, the sound echoing as they stepped through the door and into another room. Persephone hadn't seen any of Aidon's chambers except the bedroom. This room had a large pool in the corner, a natural hot spring that bubbled quietly, and behind it, the wall was completely mirrored. There were soft places to rest, all the fabric either black or a deep blood red. They went through another door into a hallway and Aidon locked it after them.

The floor was cold under Persephone's feet, the black onyx surface reflecting the orange glow of the torches lit along the passageway. These were real torches—she felt the heat of them as they passed. Hecate and Aidon seemed to know exactly where to go, but Persephone couldn't keep track of all the twists and turns, the countless number of closed doors. What went on behind them?

Persephone was completely turned around by the time she followed Aidon into the Chamber of Judgment, and she was glad Hecate hadn't let go of her hand. She recognized the room with its obsidian walls and the eerie glow of the Cypress tree. She saw three men sitting in judgment, each on his own ebony throne, at the front of the room. Aidon's larger throne was empty, but two shades wandered near it.

"There they are…" Hecate pointed to the shades by Aidon's throne. "Kometes and Prothous, the sons of Thestios."

"Both of them?" Aidon frowned. "Please don't tell me they were killed by a family member?"

Hecate smirked. "Their nephew—Meleager." The dark-haired goddess leaned down and murmured to Persephone, "Tisi makes it her personal mission to avenge familial bloodlust."

Aidon snorted. "That's an understatement—you might as well say Hera's a little jealous." He approached the two shades, two older men who began to speak at once. Persephone shook her head, as if to clear it. She couldn't understand the language of the dead, and their words sounded like wails to her ears.

"What are they saying?" She leaned in to ask Hecate and gasped when the goddess disappeared. *I can still feel her hand in mine!* Persephone started when an old woman wearing a black cloak and hood appeared in the young goddess' place. "Who are you?"

The old woman laughed. "It is me, precious—Hecate. This is the form the shades know, so it's the one I assume when I speak to them."

Persephone gaped at the old woman. Yes, she saw the resemblance, around the eyes and in the shape of the woman's jaw.

"I am the triple goddess," Hecate explained as she watched Aidon consulting with the two shades. "I can assume three forms—maiden, mother, or crone."

Persephone looked back and forth between Aidon and the old woman. "I think I like this one."

Hecate laughed—cackled, really. "Not such competition for your new lover's attention in this form, am I?" The old woman squeezed Persephone's hand. "I have no designs on him. Besides, he seems only to have eyes for you."

Even as Aidon spoke to the two men, he kept glancing over to where Persephone stood, his eyes glowing darker every time he looked at her. Hecate pulled her closer so they stood by Aidon's side.

"Does this have anything to do with the damned Calydonian Boar Artemis let loose?" Aidon asked with a sigh.

"The young hero Meleager offered the boar hide to his mistress," Hecate explained to Persephone. "His uncles here took great offense to the prize being given to a woman."

Persephone frowned. "So Meleager killed his uncles?"

"I'm afraid so." Hecate shrugged, turning to Aidon. "I told Kometes and Prothous you might grant them admission to Elysium." Hecate used her heatless torch to point to each shade in turn.

"Elysium?" Aidon gaped at her. "It is reserved only for the greatest heroes and—" Both men began to wail loudly and Persephone covered her ears. Aidon sighed, holding up his hand. "I meant no offense, but—"

Hecate, much shorter now in her old-age appearance, stretched up to Aidon to whisper, "Tisi will never think to look for them there, will she?"

The realization dawned on Aidon's face and he shook his finger at the old woman. "You are too sly for your own good, Hecate." He turned to the shades. "So be it! Off to Elysium with you both!" The two shades didn't have to be told twice. They lost themselves in a sea of shades before Persephone could even turn her head to seek them out.

"Well, that settles that." Aidon looked pleased as he slipped his arm around Persephone's waist. His large hand massaged her hip as he pulled her close and his eyes darkened again when he looked down at her. "Shall we go back to bed?"

She smiled up at him and blushed. "I wouldn't say no."

"Hades!" A man on one of the three thrones was waving to him.

"Minos!" Aidon sighed, waving back, and gave her an apologetic look. "I guess duty calls after all. Hecate, will you show Persephone around? I'll catch up with you both later."

He didn't wait for Hecate's response. Pulling Persephone to him, he kissed her—long and hard and full of lust. His tongue pressed hers, teasing, making her knees weak when he let her go. She stumbled and Hecate's hand caught her arm as Aidon winked at them both.

"Just something to remember me by." He squeezed Persephone's behind as he walked past, making her jump in surprise.

"I thought Hades was the God of the Underworld?" Persephone frowned at Hecate as she watched him approach the three smaller thrones.

"Those are just the judges." Hecate's voice had changed and Persephone turned to find yet another woman standing beside her. "Minos, Aeacus, and Rhadamanthus."

Startled, Persephone stared at the goddess' full hips and thick waist. Her face became rounder, too, softer, and definitely older than her maiden form, but much younger than the crone. "You change form faster than Zeus when he's running from Hera's wrath! This is the mother-goddess, then?"

"Yes. I like to keep everyone on their toes." Hecate winked. "Besides, you should know all my forms, as Queen of the Underworld."

Persephone stared at her for a moment. The thought of being Queen of anything hadn't really been at the forefront of her mind since she'd been brought here. "I suppose…there's a lot I should know…as Queen of the Underworld?"

"When the mortals die, they come here to be judged." Hecate explained as she took Persephone's hand and pointed toward the three smaller thrones where Aidon stood deep into conversation with one of the old men. "They were all appointed by Zeus after their deaths as judges here in the Underworld."

"I see. And I understand the pool of forgetfulness," Persephone said as they walked beneath the tall, white-lit cypress tree between the two deep pools. "But I still don't understand what the pool of memory is for."

"Ah, the Elysian Mysteries…" Hecate hesitated, stopping between the two pools. Shades slipped into the ghostly water of the Pool of Lethe, their faces sad, eyes pained. "Our ways must seem so strange to you."

"A bit," Persephone admitted, watching as the shades emerged from the pool of forgetfulness, the pain in their eyes disappearing the moment they stepped out and headed through one of the three tunnels at the end of the cavern.

"That is the crossroads," Hecate explained when she saw Persephone looking at the tunnels. "I am the goddess whose torch lights their way." The dark-haired goddess raised her torch with a smile.

"Aidon hasn't had a lot of time to explain…" Persephone apologized, hiding her blush as she turned to glance back at Aidon, who was now sitting on his throne and talking to another shade. They hadn't had much time outside of the bedroom until today. Hecate smiled and nodded her understanding, her eyes showing she knew very well Aidon hadn't given Persephone much of an explanation.

"Most of these mortals will be judged and sent to the Plains of Asphodel." Hecate nodded toward the tunnel in the middle where many of the shades crowded through the entrance. "They no longer remember their old lives and will experience neither joy nor sorrow there."

"Aidon didn't show me that place." To Persephone, they looked like zombies, their memories gone, their lives forgotten, trudging their way single-file toward an eternity of gray and colorless existence. Much like their lives, she thought, frowning.

"I imagine he didn't show you Tartarus, either." Hecate nodded her dark head toward the tunnel on the left that glimmered with a fiery orange flicker at its entrance. Aside from the eerie white of the Cypress tree, it was the only glow of light in the cavern. "It is the true hell, for those who have led very wicked lives. Not many end up there."

"I should hope not." Persephone shivered, rubbing her hands over her arms, although she wasn't really cold.

Hecate pointed toward the last tunnel, the one on the right. "But it's also true too few mortals find their way to Elysium…"

Persephone remembered the beautiful fields Aidon had shown her, so like the ones at home. Home. It was a word that made her suddenly miss her mother. A stab of homesickness overwhelmed her as she watched a few of the shades enter the tunnel that led to Elysium.

"I wish more could reside there." Persephone sighed. "It's so beautiful…so perfect…very much like my own home…"

Hecate nodded in understanding. "But many who experience the Elysian Mysteries will find their way home again. That's the purpose of the Pool of Mnemosyne."

"Memory…" Persephone stared at the shining, empty pool. "But what do they remember?"

"Their eternal nature." Hecate took Persephone's hand and they began walking again. "When mortals are born, they pass through the Moray, the three Fates, and then the river of forgetfulness. They do not know their destiny, although they are compelled to fulfill it."

"But no mortal is allowed into the Underworld," Persephone said, nodding toward the shades.

"Oh, only their spirits venture here," Hecate explained. "The pool always appears empty, but that is because it is their souls and not their bodies that enter and remember. Unlike the shades, they are completely aware and understand the significance of their Underworld journey."

"And they are the Initiates?" Persephone asked. "The ones who end up in the Elysian Fields?"

Hecate nodded. "Yes. Many of them do…along with the heroic and the virtuous. Unfortunately, among mortals there are few of either."

"Isn't that the truth?" A masculine voice interrupted them. "Don't tell me this delicious creature is our illustrious leader's new bride?"

"Persephone, this is Thanatos." Hecate sighed as she introduced them. "The God of Death."

"I'd heard you were beautiful, but words don't do you justice!" Thanatos took her hand and kissed it, and Persephone stared at his bent head in surprise. He was as light-haired and fair as she! This was the great God of Death? But when he lifted his face and smiled brightly at her, he revealed rows of gleaming teeth that made her stomach lurch when she saw them.

"Th—thank you." Persephone pulled her hand quickly away from his mouth. "I have to admit, I didn't expect Death to be so…charming."

He winked at her. "I surprise a lot of people." When he laughed at his own joke, Persephone took another step back, edging closer to Hecate. His teeth gleamed, impossibly sharp, and there had to be hundreds—thousands—lined up in close, pointed rows. "I'm about to surprise one, now. I'm heading down to Tartarus to chain a particularly nasty mortal in hell for the rest of eternity. Do you two want to come?" He said it as if inviting them to a great party.

Persephone swallowed, looking between them. "I…uh—"

"Not this time." Hecate winked at Thanatos. "I think we need to ease our bright beauty into the ways of the Underworld a little at a time."

"Are you sure?" Thanatos cocked his head at them, his blue eyes incredulous. He made it sound as if they were passing up the chance of a lifetime. "This Sisyphus character is one of the most despicable, devious, dishonest—"

"I'm sure he's lots of other D-words, too, Thannie!" Tisi came up behind them, her own fangs flashing brightly as she smiled and slapped the God of Death on the back. "Including 'disappearing' if you don't get a move on, huh?"

Thanatos bared his teeth at her and growled. "He's in Tartarus, love. Where do you think he's going to go? Home?"

"I'm just sayin'." Tisi held up her clawed hand, waving him away. "I wouldn't leave my mortals unattended."

Thanatos snorted. "He's dead, darlin'. He shuffled loose the ol' mortal coil, oh, about two hours ago." He rubbed his hands together and grinned. "Now it's just a matter of deciding his punishment."

"Let me guess—chains?" Tisi rolled her eyes at Persephone and tried to hide her words behind her hand. "He's so unimaginative."

"What's wrong with chains?" Thanatos frowned. "They're a classic, I'll have you know!" He flashed a toothy smile at Persephone. "It was nice to meet you, goddess. I do have to go find my charge, but I'm sure I'll see you around!" They all watched as he headed into the tunnel on the left, which glowed a fiery orange.

"Good to see you changed your mind about the place." Tisi's fangs showed as she smiled at Persephone. "I saw you and came over to introduce you to my sisters…this is Meg…and Alec…" The two quiet Furies behind her bowed their heads full of snakes instead of hair. Persephone still hadn't gotten used to the hissing sound or the writhing sight as each slender serpent undulated. Meg's were a deep, dark red, as were her wings. Alec's were strangely white, a bright sight down in the darkness.

"Nice to meet you." Persephone held her hand out to each of them as they bowed before her. She couldn't help leaning back away from the snakes, even though she knew they wouldn't harm her, and Tisi grinned.

"So, Hec," Tisi turned to the dark-haired goddess. "Are you showing the new Mrs. Underworld around?"

"New?" Persephone raised her eyebrows and glanced over at Aidon's throne. He was still in conversation with a shade.

Hecate rolled her eyes. "Don't let her fool you. Aidon doesn't take many women to his chambers."

"Not for lack of trying, though, right, Hec?" Tisi grinned and winked at the dark-haired goddess, whose red face was slowly fading in and out, along with the rest of her body.

"You always assume the worst, Tisi." Hecate's form appeared solid again for a moment, then shimmered out. Persephone blinked and she was back again. "There never has been anything between me and Aidon—"

"I know." Tisi nodded, clasping her hands behind her back. "Like I said, not for lack—"

"Did you all hear about Atalanta and Meleager?" Meg's voice broke into her sister's sentence, the red snakes on her head hissing in unison. Tisi gave her a dark look, but Meg went on, ignoring the dark fury on her sister's face.

"Meleager?" Persephone frowned. The name was familiar. Wasn't he the young hero who had killed his uncles? Kometes and Prothous, yes—Hecate had just suggested Aidon send them to Elysium! Persephone opened her mouth to say something, but Hecate grabbed her arm, her eyes wide, and shook her head almost imperceptibly. The dark-haired goddess' eyes went quickly and pointedly to Tisi, and Persephone remembered how much Tisi hated family violence.

"Atalanta is one of Artemis' girls, Meg." Tisi scoffed and waved her sister's gossip away. "She wouldn't touch a man with a ten foot pole."

"She touched him with more than that." Alec grinned, her white wings spreading wide.

"It's true." Meg nodded. "He's so gone on her he took her on the Calydonian Boar Hunt!"

"Well, she is a fierce huntress," Persephone remarked. They all looked at her and she flushed. "I...know Artemis well. I met Atalanta a few times. They were very close."

"See?" Tisi frowned. "This Meleager may be gone on Atalanta, but she—"

"Your sister speaks the truth." Hecate was now back to her maiden form, her long dark hair hardly covering her bare breasts. Persephone blinked, shaking her head. Her changing was very disconcerting.

"How do you know?" Tisi crossed her arms and rolled her eyes.

"I swear, it's true!" Meg's red wings quivered in agitation. "Atalanta has fallen in love with the youngest of the Argonauts and has killed the Calydonian Boar!"

"Meleager's married," Tisi reminded her with a frown. "And I could care less about the stupid boar."

Hecate snorted. "When has that ever stopped a man? She's right, Tisi. I heard it from Zeus myself."

"Really?" The dark Fury sighed. "Well, there goes my hope for humanity."

Meg grinned. "Like you had any to begin with. I hear they're very much in love."

"In lust is more like it." Alec rolled her eyes. "I heard they both nearly got trampled by the boar when they were out trysting in the woods. That's how they caught it."

"Sounds like they got caught themselves," Tisi snorted. "I have no sympathy for adulterers. The only thing worse is someone who would kill their own family." Her sharp fangs showed in a sneer and Persephone swallowed hard, glancing at Hecate. "Now I'm in the mood to torture someone. Hey,

Meggie, weren't you telling me about some woman who killed her child and fed it to her sister's husband?"

Meg nodded, shrugging and giving Hecate an apologetic look when the goddess waved her hands behind Tisi's back, trying to quiet her. "Her husband raped her sister and cut out her tongue…so she took revenge by killing her own child and feeding him to her husband…"

"Now there's a woman who's got some imagination." Tisi winked at Persephone. "Let's go, Furies. We've got work to do."

The three of them took off at once, their wings spread wide—a flurry of white, red and black—as they sailed toward the exit. Persephone turned to stare open-mouthed at Hecate. No wonder the goddess had gone out of her way to keep Meleager's poor uncles' deaths from the Fury!

Hecate sighed and, as if reading Persephone's mind, said, "If Tisi even got a whiff of what Meleager did to his uncles, the young hero would be doomed. Hopefully, she'll never think to look for them in Elysium."

Persephone glanced toward Aidon, who had made the decision to send the two shades to their eternal fate in order to keep a young man from Tisi's wrath. He was still engrossed in conversation. "This place…is very different."

"It takes some getting used to." Hecate nodded sympathetically. "So—which tunnel would you like to explore, goddess?" She waved her torch toward the three—Tartarus, Asphodel, and Elysium.

"I've had enough of death and sadness." Persephone made a face. "Take me back to Elysium. It's more like my home."

The dark-haired goddess took her hand and together they headed toward the entrance to heaven.

Chapter Four

"This soooo reminds me of home." Persephone stretched her arms toward the sunless sky and danced in the field of wildflowers. Her golden hair streamed behind her as she twirled, laughing and collapsing next to Hecate, who was watching quietly while leaning against a tree.

"Do you miss your home?" Hecate patted the ground beside her and Persephone wiggled next to the dark-haired goddess. She was in her maiden form again, her black hair shining almost blue in the light. The simulation of a summer day was nearly perfect, except for the absence of sun and clouds. The light was bright, warm, and there was even a gentle breeze blowing the golden groundsel against their bare ankles, just like home.

"Yes, I do miss it." Persephone sighed, looking across the field and remembering her mother's home, her mother's smile, the warm smell of bread baking as she came home from an afternoon picking flowers. She knew she had missed the festival, and all of the fun. She wondered if Demeter had cancelled it when she discovered her daughter missing. She must be worried sick. Persephone tried to shove the thought away, shading her eyes to see at a man and woman coupling in the distance. "Although, I have to admit, we didn't have sights quite like these at home."

Hecate chuckled. "I imagine not. There are no inhibitions here in the Underworld. Yet another thing it will take you time to get used to, no doubt."

"I'm learning." Persephone winked, looking down at her own nude form, and then at Hecate's. Walking around naked was incredibly freeing, she discovered. She felt proud of her body in ways she never had before—especially when Aidon looked at her. No humans resided here to ogle her, like men did back home whenever she chanced upon them. She knew Demeter had been right to worry, to give her the necklace for protection. But down here, she had no need for the charm of her mother's love—she had Aidon. She was, ironically, safer from prying eyes down here than she ever had been when she was living with her mother. The shades were only drawn to one another, and the rest of the Underworld crowd seemed to understand Aidon's word as law.

"What do you miss?" Hecate inquired.

"The sun." Persephone looked up at the bright sky. It seemed impossible not to see the sun blazing there, or clouds drifting by. "I even miss the rain…"

"There is no weather here," Hecate admitted. "Just light turning to darkness and back again."

"I used to dream of Elysium." Persephone twisted the strands of sweet grass she had picked into an intricate braid. "Magical forever springtime."

"Forbidden springtime?" Hecate raised an eyebrow in her direction.

Persephone blushed. "Am I so transparent?"

"Not as transparent as most of the folks around here." Hecate laughed at her joke, nodding toward two shades passing by, holding hands. "But I'm a pretty good intuitive."

"It is magical." Persephone's eyes skipped over the expanse of meadow. "Amazing. It's almost perfect. Almost. But there's something that isn't quite the same…"

Hecate nodded. "I know. Being a twain-traveler, I come and go—here, up there, Mount Olympus. You name it, I've been there."

"Which do you like best?" Persephone stopped braiding, tilting her golden head toward the other goddess.

"I don't like to pick favorites." Hecate winked, giving her a smile. "But I have to say…the Underworld has its charms."

"Like Aidon?" Persephone smiled dreamily.

"He is charming." Hecate laughed. "You like him, don't you?"

"Don't you?"

"I do," Hecate admitted with a sigh. "He is quite maligned and misunderstood, I think."

Persephone shrugged, remembering her own reaction to the God of the Underworld showing up in her meadow. "Perhaps."

"There is no other God I know who is as fair and just as Aidon." Hecate pulled her knees up to her chest, resting her chin there. "I respect him a great deal."

"I do like him." Persephone smiled, remembering the way he looked at her. "This has all happened so quickly...I've hardly had time to think about it."

"You just need some time to get used to us..." Hecate picked one of the violets, twirling the purple flower in her fingers. "To him."

"I guess so." Persephone sighed, tossing her sweet grass braid on the ground. "Going home isn't an option."

Hecate retrieved the twisted grass, weaving the violet's stem into it. "But you miss it?"

"Yes," Persephone admitted, leaning her head back against the trunk of the tree and closing her eyes. "Although...I'm beginning to wonder..." Her voice trailed off and she sighed. Whenever she thought of home, she couldn't help thinking of her mother. Athena and Artemis surely scoured the surrounding woods for her, and Demeter, she knew, would be beside herself. Still...

She spoke the soft words mostly to herself. "Perhaps I miss it because that's what I'm expected to do?"

"But whose expectations are they?" Hecate's response made Persephone jump and open her eyes again. The coupling shades rolled in the grass, and their laughter carried on the wind. She found herself thinking of Aidon.

"My mother's expectations, I suppose..." she answered finally. "When Aidon first brought me here, I was afraid. And then..."

"Then?" Hecate prompted, nudging the goddess with her knee. "How do you really feel, Persephone? About Aidon? About the Underworld?"

She turned her face up to the sky. There was no sun, and yet the warmth was inviting. It reminded her of the way

Aidon looked at her—the heat of his gaze was like that—light and dark all at once. "I guess I'm not really sure." Persephone looked over at Hecate and frowned at her own realization. "I don't think I've ever had the opportunity to make up my own mind about much of anything."

Hecate smiled, brushing a strand of golden hair away from the goddess' face. "Well, now you have your chance."

Persephone swallowed, looking down at the ground. For all she kept insisting to the world she wasn't a child, she had certainly never done anything to prove otherwise. She glanced over at the dark-haired goddess, frowning. "Listen, I'm not keeping you from anything, am I?" She gestured to Hecate's torch stuck into the ground by her side, the light dimmer here. "I really don't need a babysitter."

Hecate gave her an understanding smile. "I actually do have things to do…" She stood, shaking grass out of her hair and picking up her torch. "Do you know your way back?"

"I'll be fine," Persephone insisted, jutting her chin out. "I'm a big girl."

"Yes. You are." Hecate leaned over and kissed the top of Persephone's head. "If you need anything, just call me. I'll pop right back." With that, the goddess disappeared. One moment she was there, and the next she was simply gone.

Persephone blinked at the space Hecate had vacated and muttered, "She wasn't kidding."

Standing, she decided to go for a walk across the fields, toward a little path that showed just at the edge of the woods. The trees made it cooler as she made her way down the trail, and she heard the sound of running water. She followed it for a distance and came to a stream with a soft, grassy bank. *This is just like home!* Stunned at the resemblance, she suddenly remembered the man she had seen in the woods and flushed. She had been innocent then, a virgin still, fascinated by her own lust.

Persephone stretched out on the grass, dipping just her feet into the cooling water of the stream. Her thoughts filled with Aidon. He had come for her, taken her, beaten her, bound her, ravished her… She knew she should be outraged, repulsed, even scandalized—but she wasn't. Everything she had ever felt seemed like a "should" to her. Her mother would be disgraced, Athena and Artemis outraged and even sickened. But Persephone, the Goddess of Spring simply longed for more.

I want him. The realization was sudden and sent a sweet jolt of sensation down to her core. The feeling she had for the man by the stream was no different than the feeling she had for Aidon! It was lust; that was all. The realization was a shameful relief. His hold over her was just pure animal desire, nothing more. She couldn't be blamed for her own body's response to him, could she?

The memory of him entering her for the first time made her moan out loud. The press of his flesh into her compared to the cold, buzzing phallus Athena had used was the difference between the Underworld and Olympus. There was a fire, a dark heat, in the coming together of their flesh that the unyielding, implacable golden phallus couldn't possibly simulate.

Glancing around to make sure she was alone, Persephone's hand drifted down to her sex. Her lips were already swollen, parting slightly in invitation to her fingers. She pressed one, then two, deep into that no-longer-virgin orifice, remembering the stiff length of him there. She wanted more and slipped in a third, but it still couldn't approximate the thick feel of Aidon filling her. Sliding her fingers in and out, she used her thumb at the top of her cleft to rub her aching little omi.

"Aidon," she whispered, pumping her hand faster. Her nipples hardened in her excitement, the breeze over them felt almost like a tender kiss. The sensation sent delicious shivers down between her thighs. Her thumb strummed up and down, her fingers slipping in and out, and the soft, wet sensation on her breast sent her spiraling ever closer to her climax. She was too close to wonder about it, her hips arching skyward as she sent herself over the edge, imagining Aidon filling her again and again.

It was only as she was coming back down to earth that she realized the gentle licking at her breast hadn't stopped. Startled, Persephone opened her eyes and sat up with a gasp. There's no one here… She was still alone by the stream, and yet when she touched her nipple, it was wet with a residue she knew was saliva. How?

Glancing around, she frowned. "Aidon?" she whispered, and although it seemed impossible, she could feel him, sense him, somewhere near. She heard a deep chuckle, one she had become intimately familiar with, and suddenly Aidon materialized beside her, pulling his golden helmet off his dark head.

"Surprise." He grinned, putting the helmet beside him on the grass and leaning in to kiss her. His lips moved, warm and soft, his mouth a gentle exploration. When they parted, she stared at him in wonder as he traced the line of her jaw with his finger. "Do you have any idea how beautiful you are, touching yourself like that?"

"It was you?" She touched the helmet between them.

"The invisibility helmet comes in handy." He grinned again and winked.

"That's not a nice trick." She frowned at him, crossing her arms over her chest.

He chuckled. "I'm not nice."

She squealed as he pulled her into his lap, wrapping her legs around his waist and squeezing her tight. His hold was so strong she struggled to breathe as she twisted in his grip. His hands grasped her behind, grinding her into him, and she could feel how hard he was under his loincloth. He found her lips again, giving her a hard, relentless kiss that left her dazed and dizzy when they parted.

"Hecate says you're just maligned and misunderstood," Persephone murmured, meeting his eyes with a smile.

Aidon shook his head. "Nah. Malevolent and maladjusted. That's more me." He grabbed her hair in his hands, tilting her head back and drizzling kisses down her throat. "Haven't you heard the stories about Hades, the God of the Dead?"

She moaned softly, tightening her legs around him. "Yes. They say you're a beast, a brute…"

"It's true." Aidon's grip tensed in her hair as his tongue traced circles downward to her breasts. "Go on."

"You're…" Her words trailed off as his tongue found her nipple and she arched it toward his mouth. "Oh…Aidon…they say you're…a fiend…a monster…"

"All true." He rolled her onto her back, and she felt the heated length of his erection between her legs, separated only by the thin material, as he sucked her nipple deep into his mouth. Persephone squirmed under his weight, running her hands down his shoulders and arms. "What else?"

"Oh!" Her gasp of surprise that his loincloth had somehow disappeared was swallowed by his kiss when their tongues met. He slid the head of his erection up and down between her swollen nether lips, making her moan and lift her hips to meet him.

"What else do they say about me, Sephie?" He murmured the words into her ear as he sank slowly into her flesh, parting her with his thick length.

"This is what I wanted." She took all of him and wiggled up for more. "They say…you love sighs…"

He met her eyes, thrusting slowly in and out now. "Yes."

"And tears."

He nodded, his eyes dark as he moved. "Yes." He ground himself deep into her, grabbing her wrists and pinning them over her head. "Especially yours."

"Aidon!" she gasped as he took her, impaling her again and again. She was helpless to his lust as he bucked, crushing her with his weight. The delicious friction was undeniable, and she moaned and rocked with him, aching for more. "Aidon, please!"

"Yes!" he growled into her ear. "Beg me."

"Please!" she moaned, digging her heels into the small of his back. "Don't stop!"

He groaned at her words, moving his hips in fast circles that sent her shuddering into her climax in no time. She twisted and quivered beneath him as he filled her—she could feel every hot pulse—with surge after surge of his thick, white seed.

She welcomed his weight as he collapsed onto her, his breathing slowing in her ear. His heart still beat hard against hers, and she sighed when she felt him soften and slip out of her. She wiggled and felt the sticky mess he'd left slipping down toward the ground below.

"See how evil I am?" he chuckled, rolling off her onto the grass.

"You are both wicked and depraved." She smiled up into the trees. "I think I like it."

"You think?" He snorted, rolling toward her and slipping his hand between her thighs to cover her mound. "Perhaps you need another example in order to make up your mind?"

Persephone laughed, wiggling out from under his hand and wading into the stream. "You made me all dirty! Now I need a bath." She sank down into the water up to her waist, piling her hair up onto her head. Aidon waded in after her, smiling as he pulled her against him and kissed her.

"You drive me to distraction, Sephie." He looked down at her, shaking his head. "I couldn't help but follow you."

She blinked up at him. "Follow? How long have you been here?"

"Since..." He shrugged, averting his gaze. "Let's just say, I heard most of your conversation with Hecate."

"You are evil!" She beat his chest with her small fists. "Spying on us like that!"

"I had to make sure you were behaving." He caught her wrists, his laughing eyes suddenly turning serious. "Do you really miss your home?"

Persephone sighed and shook her head. "I don't know."

"I know the Underworld is…different." He kissed the top of her golden head. "But it isn't just darkness. Look around you, goddess. This is springtime all year round, the embodiment of the joy of those mortals who lived a good life." Persephone breathed deep, taking in her surroundings. He was right—it was beautiful. Just as beautiful as her own home. "There is balance in everything here. Mortals are rewarded or punished based on what they deserve. This is heaven and hell all at once. The Underworld is what you make of it."

"I know, Aidon. It's just…" She lifted her eyes to his. "Maybe I just needed time to say goodbye?"

He frowned, looking thoughtful. "To your mother?"

"No!" Persephone's eyes widened. "We both know she wouldn't approve of…us. I'd rather her not know, I think."

Aidon nodded. "I understand."

"But…" She rested her head against his chest with sigh. "I am the Goddess of Spring, after all. I can't help it. I miss my meadows, my fields, my streams."

He held her for a moment, the water rushing around their bare legs. Then he tilted her chin up to his. "Would you like to go visit?"

Her eyes brightened. "Home?"

He nodded. "No one could see you, but you could walk in your meadow and wade in your stream…say goodbye to your world."

"Yes, please." She blinked back tears, a lump forming in her throat. Raising his hand, she kissed his palm, cradling it to her cheek. "Thank you, Aidon."

He just nodded, giving the sharp, distinctive whistle that would call Noire, the big black steed, to carry them out of the Underworld.

* * * *

Persephone adjusted the invisibility helmet on her head as she slid off Noire's back onto the sweet, familiar grass of her home. Aidon had already dismounted and she took his hand. He started, looking down to where she should have been standing, were she visible to the naked eye.

"That's decidedly disconcerting." He frowned, squeezing her hand.

"It is, isn't it?" She laughed. Her voice was audible, and she pulled him along through the field of wildflowers, where they left Noire grazing. "Look, Aidon, this is where you found me."

Persephone recognized the small clearing where she and the other goddesses had often rested in the heat of the sun. She remembered the necklace she had left there, and squatted down, running her hand through the grass where it had been. She wondered if her mother had found it. Or perhaps Athena or Artemis, coming by after the hunt? There was no sign of the locket on its gold chain.

She stood, picking wildflowers and tucking them into her hair, humming to herself. The day was bright but slightly colder than it should have been, she noticed. Helios seemed to struggle to stay blazing in the sky, and dark clouds competed for space in the blue expanse above. Breathing deep, she smiled and took Aidon's hand again.

"Could you at least warn me?" he asked after giving a short yelp of surprise.

She giggled. "That would be more than you gave me, wouldn't it?" Squeezing his hand, she led him along, heading toward the path toward the stream.

"I saw a woodsman bathing here the day you found me," she confessed, sitting down by the stream and pulling him with her. Her invisibility seemed to give her the courage to say things she normally wouldn't.

Aidon raised his eyebrows. "Did you?"

"He was…" She cleared her throat, glad her lack of visibility hid her blush. "Touching himself…down there."

"Was he?" Aidon glanced across the stream. "And you stayed to watch?"

Persephone blushed and nodded before she remembered he couldn't see her. "I was curious…about men."

He smirked. "And how did you feel after you watched him?"

"More curious." She grinned, remembering.

"And have I satisfied your curiosity?"

She looked up at him, studying his face. He couldn't see her watching him, and she had the freedom to explore him with her eyes. His form fascinated her—the broad shoulders, his ridged, flat stomach, the thick muscles in his thighs. "I don't know if my curiosity will ever be satisfied."

"For men?" he snorted.

She shook her head. "For you."

His startled look made her smile and she stood, letting go of his hand.

"Persephone?" he called, frowning. "Don't wander off."

"I need to go get something." She leaned down and kissed his cheek lightly. "I'll be right back. Stay here."

He called to her, but she skipped down the path, around a bend to another small clearing. Here several trees grew, heavy with fruit, and she plucked two of her ripe favorites— the pomegranate. There was something about the flavor, the way sweet, ripe fruit enveloped the hard, bitter seeds. It was the combination of the bitter and sweet flavor she loved.

She wandered back to where she had left Aidon, imagining feeding pomegranate seeds into his waiting mouth. The trail was familiar, the trees and plants and flowers all hers, but she realized that they held less attraction for now. They were beautiful certainly—but so was Elysium. And there was a darkness in the Underworld she had discovered she craved, something…bittersweet.

This really is goodbye.

The thought of leaving this place for the Underworld didn't make her sad. The sound of the stream around the bend was music to her ears and she turned the corner, opening her mouth to call him. Aidon was on his back with a dark-haired nymph straddling his chest. Persephone recognized her immediately. Nymphs were always tied to particular locations, and this stream belonged to Minthe.

The beautiful seductress, who had lured many a man and god in her time, was now leaning down to kiss the God of the Underworld.

"Get off of him!" Persephone shrieked, dropping her fruit and pulling the invisibility helmet off her head. Minthe glanced up, her dark eyes wide in surprise. Aidon pushed her off in that moment, using all of his strength, and the nymph went sprawling on the ground.

"She bewitched me!" Aidon wiped the dazed look from his face. "I could have sworn she was you, Sephie!"

Persephone's eyes narrowed and she looked between them, frowning. She didn't know how far the nymph's powers reached, or what tricks she was capable of, but the confused look in Aidon's eyes made things clearer.

"Well, Minthe..." Persephone turned, glaring at the nymph, and raised both hands to her. "You won't have the chance to do that again." A flash of heat emitted from Persephone and Minthe's beautiful form was transformed in an instant. Aidon stared, mouth agape, his eyes going from his bride to the sudden appearance of a small bush with spiky purple flowers where Minthe had been standing.

"I'm sorry, Sephie," he apologized, taking her in his arms. She let him, still shaking with rage. "At first she said she had lost her way...and then, when she climbed onto me, she took your form somehow."

She glanced up at him, still frowning. "Did you think her beautiful?"

"Yes." Aidon cleared his throat when he saw the look on her face. "But—"

"I think she is more beautiful now." Persephone spoke firmly as she went over to the plant, picking off one of the leaves. "And she smells better. Here." Aidon lifted the pungent smelling leaves to his nose. "Minthe will serve much better this way, don't you think?"

Aidon chuckled, picking up the helmet she had discarded. "I never expected to see such a display of jealousy from you."

Persephone crossed her arms over her chest. "I'm not jealous. That nymph was a menace. I was just doing a public service."

"If you say so." Aidon hid a smile, leaning down to pick up one of the fruits she had dropped. "Pomegranates? Is this what you went wandering off for?"

"They're my favorites." Persephone sighed, coming over to stand beside him. "I was bringing them back to—oh, never mind." She glanced over at the newly sprung mint plant swaying in the breeze, taking the pomegranate from his hand and tossing it at the shrub. Its leaves shook violently at the blow. "Let's just go home."

Aidon's eyebrow went up. "Home?"

"You heard me." Persephone took his hand and they headed back up the path to find Noire to carry them back to the Underworld.

Chapter Five

The knock on the door startled them both and Aidon swore softly, getting up off the bed and padding nude toward the door. "Who is it? This better be good!"

"It's Tisi!" She sounded apologetic. "I wouldn't have bothered you, but—"

"Damn it, Tisi!" He pulled open the door and Persephone strained to see from her reclining position on the bed. Tisi grinned down at his fading erection and then peeked past his shoulder, seeing Persephone strapped to the bed. "I told you we were not to be disturbed!"

"I know, but Thanatos—"

"The God of Death is a big boy! I'm sure he can take care of himself!" Aidon turned her around by the wings, pushing her forward through the outer chamber. Persephone couldn't see them anymore, but she could hear them.

"Aidon, wait—"

"No!" His voice echoed loudly. "The damned Underworld can live without me for a few days! Now go, and don't disturb me again!"

Persephone winced when the door slammed shut and Aidon stormed back in, still swearing at Tisi under his breath. He stopped short, standing to the side and looking at the goddess displayed spread-eagle on his bed. She could see the fire beginning again in his eyes. There was a definite difference between the glow of anger and the spark of passion in his deep smoldering gaze. She had time to marvel she had already learned the difference before Aidon climbed up on the bed beside her.

"Now...where were we?"

She was chained to the bed with padded wrist and ankle restraints, completely at his mercy. She squirmed under the intensity of his gaze, his eyes slowly tracing a path over her skin. There was no mistaking his look now, the heat of it making her skin flush. He propped himself up on his elbow and traced a finger around her navel, making easy, concentric circles out from her center. Persephone longed to reach for him, but with her hands bound, she just wiggled in her restraints, giving a small whimper.

He didn't pay any attention to her writhing. Instead, he lowered his mouth to her navel and kissed her, tracing his tongue in the same circles his fingers had made. She shivered at the hot, wet trail he left on her skin, arching her hips up without even thinking. The feel of his hand on her knee, petting her there before moving up over the swell of her thigh, made her moan softly, her head rolling slowly from side to side.

The wet circles moved inward again, his fingers brushing lightly over the skin of her inner thigh. His touch was feather-soft, his tongue slipping into the crevice of her navel. She gasped at the sensation, surprised at her own response. It was as if he were licking her lower, in the more sensitive nether regions of her sex! His tongue dipped in and out, moving around and around, making her squirm. She could swear she felt it all where his fingers stroked her inner thighs.

"Please..." The word escaped her lips in a hoarse whisper as she twisted against her restraints. It was as if he hadn't heard her at all. His tongue continued its slow exploration of her waistline, his fingers their agonizing tease. He was clearly doing what he wanted, what suited him at that moment. He kissed down her belly, the mattress shifting under his weight as he settled himself between her thighs.

She tensed in anticipation, pushing her hips up toward his mouth, but his tongue began those maddening circles again, moving up from her knee to inner thigh. Just when his breath whispered where she wanted to be touched, he moved again, starting at her other knee and working his way up again. She groaned in frustration at the slow torture of his mouth, twisting her wrists in her padded bonds.

When he finally touched her sex, it wasn't with his tongue at all. His big hands pressed her thighs open wider at the apex, his fingers easing her curls apart to expose the pink inside. She lifted her head to look down at him, his gaze focused between her legs. When he looked up and met her eyes, his face spread into a slow smile.

"Athena and Artemis have a name for it," she told him, pressing her hips up. "For that sweet spot at the top, right there…"

"This one?" He pressed his finger to it briefly and she shivered.

"Yessss…ohhh." Swallowing hard, she went on, "They call it the feminine omphalos."

"The center of feminine pleasure." He touched it again, rubbing back and forth, making her moan. "Indeed."

"We called it omi."

"Well, you have a beautiful little omi, Sephie." He blew on it gently,

"Please," she whispered again, wiggling her pelvis up toward his mouth. "Oh, Aidon, please, I'm begging you…"

"I hear that." His smile widened. His finger and thumb touched the pink, sheathed hood of skin and pulled it back to expose her completely. "I like the sound of it. Do it again."

She gasped as his finger rubbed her omi back and forth, teasing. "Aidon! Oh please!"

"Again." His finger unsheathed her over and over, playing with her.

"Please!" Her voice was almost a wail. "Please, please, please!"

"Please what?" He kissed just above where his fingers pressed. "What is it you want, Sephie?"

She moaned when his breath moved over her mound. "Your mouth. Your tongue."

"Here?"

"Yes, there!" Her hips rocked up against his flickering tongue. "Oh right there!"

"Work for it." He lifted his tongue, flicking it back and forth through the air over her mound. "Let's see if you can reach for what you want."

She groaned, arching as high as she could in her restraints, toward his waiting mouth. Every time she eased a little closer to his tongue, he would pull back slightly, making her moan in frustration. Finally, she sighed, lowering her hips to the bed. The effort caused her breath to come in short, fast pants.

"Your pleasure is mine." His fingers still spread her open, exposing her. "It belongs to me. You will give it to me, if and when I want it. Do you understand?"

Whimpering, she nodded.

"I didn't hear you." He pinched her omi gently, making her squirm.

"Yes, Aidon!" Persephone's moan echoed in the room as he sank down into her flesh, his tongue probing through her soft, pink heat. There was no teasing or hesitation now. His mouth licked her most sensitive spots, his fingers working slowly into her, one at a time. He drank her in—she could hear him swallowing her—and he groaned for more, sliding his wet fingers in and out of her sex.

She longed to grab his head, press him to her harder, and she tugged at her restraints. Struggling against them was no use—her pleasure was completely his. There was nothing she could do to control it, no matter how much she twisted and turned and arched. His fingers curled up inside of her, pressing some deep, aching spot as his tongue flicked back and forth at the top of her slit.

It seemed to go on forever, his dancing tongue and crooking fingers sending her closer and closer toward her peak. Her thighs began to tremble with her impending orgasm and she felt an incredible surge between her legs, as if she were going to let everything go. Panicked, she tried to stop, but she couldn't. His mouth urged her on, his fingers, too, taking her to new heights as she bucked under him.

"No!" Her head rolled from side to side, her eyes closed tight against it, but there was no stopping whatever was coming. This wasn't like anything she had ever felt before, and it both exhilarated and bewildered her. The sensation seemed to grow wings, beginning with a soft flutter and then taking off. Soon she was soaring, her whole body humming with the delicious feeling. And he never stopped, seeking more and more of her as she shuddered and gasped against him. She could hear him swallowing, moaning softly between her legs as he drank gushes of her fluid.

When it had faded to just an aching pulse and a trickle, Aidon knelt up, his eyes dark with lust as he looked down at her. She wanted to reach for him, but couldn't. She could only show him her hunger through her eyes, the flush of her skin, the gasp of her breath. He seemed to understand it as he grabbed his erection, stroking it gently as he straddled her hips. Her eyes moved along with his hand, up and down the shaft, and she licked her lips.

"You are mine, Persephone." He slid his stiff heat under the chain linked between the nipple clamps on her breasts, letting it catch the chain as it rose and pulled slightly, making her gasp. Her nipples suddenly burned with feeling, and she watched as the head of his cock leaked fluid down toward the gold chain. "You are mine, to do with as I will. Every part of you." He thrust upward a little, pulling the chain taut. She moaned, biting her lip at the delightful pain. "Every orifice is mine." He reached behind him to grab her mound, shoving his fingers inside of her. She groaned, but the sound was muffled as he slipped the chain off his shaft and eased the tip between her lips. His fingers pressed deeper into her sex as he rocked his hips forward, shoving himself toward the back of her throat. "Every single hole...all mine." His finger slipped lower, down the crack of her behind, and she felt him pressing the tender, still-virgin rosebud below her sex. Her eyes widened, but she couldn't speak as he pressed himself further into her mouth. "And I will use them all, Sephie. What do you think of that?"

The feel of his finger probing, the thought of him touching her there, putting what was in her mouth down there...! She had thought she had seen darkness down here, since she had been taken by him, but now she was starting to realize they had just begun. The thought was both terrifying and exciting. Her response was not given in words, but by her eager suckling and swallowing of his thick shaft.

She lost herself in the thrust and growl of him pumping in and out of her mouth, but he didn't let it go on long. With a loud groan, he pulled his dripping shaft from her lips, smacking her lightly on the cheek with the head as she whimpered and tried to catch it again with her tongue.

"Bad girl." He gently slapped her other cheek with his erection before standing and moving away from the bed. Persephone strained to see what he was doing, where he was going. He opened a cupboard and pulled out all sorts of things, some she recognized, some she didn't. She turned her head as he brought an armful of things toward her, strange leather straps and sharp metal poking at odd angles. The sight of it made her breath catch.

Aidon yanked the table next to the bed closer with one hand, sweeping the metal bowl onto the floor, spilling the fruit it contained. It rolled everywhere. He dropped his armload of implements onto the bed and then began to line them up on the table, one by one. She watched, her whole body tingling with anticipation at the look of determination on his face. His gaze flicked over her and he frowned, picking up a black square of silk from the pile.

"You will come to crave the darkness." His voice was soft as he folded the cloth and slipped it over her eyes. He tied it behind her head, and she gasped when he tugged the chain still attached between her nipples. Now she couldn't see what he was doing, she could only listen as he shuffled the implements on the table. The weight of him shifted the bed slightly and she knew he was sitting beside her. She could hear his breath, and she wondered what he was doing, what he was thinking.

His hand slid up the curve of her arm toward her wrist, and she whimpered as he unlocked the restraint. She flexed and stretched her aching arm before letting it fall to the bed.

He did the same with the other arm and both legs. Persephone twisted and arched her limbs on the mattress, sighing in relief. She hadn't even realized how restricted she had been, bound to the bed that way.

"Turn over." His voice was a soft command, and she found herself rolling to her belly, complying with his directive. She was careful of the clamps on her nipples, but they bit into her flesh harder anyway as her breasts pressed against the bed. The darkness enveloped her, and with that particular sense deprived, she found her others slightly heightened. The feel of him shifting on the bed was like the earth moving. Something scraped across the table next to the bed and she turned her head sharply toward the sound. Even the smell of leather, that wild, slightly animal scent, wafting near her cheek, drew her attention.

Something cold brushed her shoulder and she shivered. She jumped at a soft "snick" sound under her chin, and Aidon jerked gently at the soft leather collar around her neck a few times before giving a satisfied grunt. Persephone opened her mouth to ask him, but his words cut off her own.

"It's a leash." Again, that gentle tug. "You're not quite ready for your freedom yet." The words burned her ears and cheeks and the impulse to run was very strong. He seemed to sense it, and the wrench on the leash grew tighter. "You chose to stay, Sephie. Now you're going to find out why. Spread your legs."

The last statement was another command, and she swallowed her pride, spreading her thighs wide on the bed. The silence seemed to go on forever as she listened to her own fast-beating heart in the darkness. She knew he was there, somewhere near, but there was no movement—just the deep, even sound of his breathing. Just when she thought she couldn't stand it any longer, she had to move or say something to break the endless silence, the softest tickle feathered over the sole of her foot.

Lightly, the sensation trailed up over her calf, twirling there in the sensitive area behind her knee. Back and forth, then, over her thighs, and up over her behind, in slow, sweeping figure eights that made her shiver with delight. Aidon swept her hair over her shoulder, teasing the back of neck with the silky sensation. The feather—she knew it must be a feather—tickled her forehead and cheek and chin, making her smile. He traced it over the side of her breast and down the gentle curve of her waist, making fast circles on her hip.

Then, out of nowhere, a bright hot sensation seared her behind. She yelped, twisting on the bed, the nipple clamps shifting and making her breasts burn. The leash attached to her collar pulled snug and she stopped, wiggling slightly but not moving any further away from the sensation. Aidon's hand moved over the burning, as if rubbing it in, or rubbing it out, she wasn't sure which. It felt incredible and she moaned softly, arching up into his palm.

He replaced his hand with that light, feathery touch, brushing softly over her bottom. The sensation sent shivery bumps down her legs and over her arms and she lifted her hips toward it. That's when something hard and soft at the same time came down fast against her flesh, its flat, padded surface making her jump with the force. She squealed as another blow fell and then another. It began slowly, teasing. Holding her breath, she waited for the next one, not sure if or when it was coming. When it did, she gasped and arched off the mattress.

There was no rhyme or reason to it, and she found herself tense with uncertainty. The next few slaps rained down hard over her behind again and again—her breath came in short gasps and she gripped the bedclothes in her fists, bracing herself—and then they stopped. She drew a long, shaky breath, turning her head, as if she could tell what he might do next, although the blindfold left her in darkness. Her whole body tingled with anticipation.

Aidon's hand smoothed the way over the flesh of her bottom for a moment, the tender touch of his hand making her shiver. Then he roughly pressed her thighs open, cupping her mound in one hand. Until that moment, she had been unaware of the dull ache between her legs. When he lifted her, bringing her to her knees on the bed, her face pressed against the mattress, his hand reminded her of her throbbing sex with a delicious pressure.

He moved away and she whimpered, wondering what was coming next. She was completely exposed to him now, her red, singing bottom wavering high up in the air. It wasn't long before he took advantage of it, his hand striking her at the bend of one thigh, hard enough to make her jump. He rubbed there for a moment and then slipped his hand down to part her with his fingers.

"Don't move." His instruction was clear and she froze, feeling a thin, hard object sliding in her wetness. His fingers moved, deft and careful, his breath warm against her thigh. The sensitive bud of her sex felt constricted, slowly squeezed by something. "This is weighted. It will feel strange at first."

She gasped as he moved his hand away and something heavy pulled downward. Too curious to stop herself, she probed her fingers between her own lips to feel something hard clamped around her omi, and several small, round smooth weights hanging from it. Aidon slapped her hand with something, a fast bee-sting feeling and she hissed, pulling away quickly.

"Hands and knees." He briefly tapped her shoulder with something, and she moved to accommodate him. The weights shifted between her legs, pulling on her sex, and she moaned softly as they swung back and forth, stimulating her omi. She didn't have long to pay attention to them, though, because Aidon used the crop—it had to be the riding crop from the table—to needle her behind again.

It was a sharp, fast pain that faded less readily as he continued to spank her. Her bottom sang with the sensation and she rocked with it, wincing and moaning at turns. Every movement she made sent the weights between her legs swinging back and forth, tickling her omi. The sweet torture went on and on, as Aidon began switching back and forth between the paddle and the crop, the soft slap and the prickle. There was no consistent pattern, and she trembled in anticipation, wondering which would come next.

Her bottom felt on fire, and the deep throbbing ache between her legs made her breath come fast and her still-clamped nipples burn. She whimpered and twisted and arched as Aidon continued his onslaught, not sure if she was seeking to get away or looking for more. Just when she thought she couldn't stand any more, he stopped.

"Aidon!" His name left her lips in a gasp when she felt his hard length against her sex. He teased her with the head, slapping at the pink flesh, and then with a low growl, he shoved inside of her. His hands gripped her hips when he pressed deep, rocking her forward as he pulled her into the saddle of his hips. He rolled against her, making circles, forcing the weights beneath her to sway, teasing her omi.

His big hands kneaded her flesh, his thumbs pressing toward the center, parting the deep crevice of her bottom. She gasped and bit her lip when his thumb pressed the puckered rosebud of her behind, made slippery with her juices and their coupling. He didn't force entry—he just rubbed it in easy turns, the kind his hips continued to make as they rocked together.

"Mine, Sephie." His tone low, his thumb pressed, slipping inside that dark, virgin hole. Her breath caught at the sensation. "Every part of you. Do you understand?"

She couldn't think, couldn't respond. Her body trembled against his, her bursting, blooming sex felt on fire, her nipples ached. His thumb probed a little deeper, forcing her open, and she whimpered, squeezing the muscles tight. Aidon groaned, suddenly slipping out of her. She didn't have time to even gasp in surprise as he rolled her over, shoving her legs back, and aimed himself again between them. The weights pulling taut on her omi went slack and her aching omi throbbed even harder in response. Somehow the tension had made her even more swollen, more sensitive.

"Mine." He rubbed her omi with his thumb as he slid himself slowly in and out of her sex, making her moan. With his other hand, he gave a gentle tug on the chain dangling between her nipples. "Mine." The chorus her body sang neared an impossible peak, and she knew she couldn't hold out any more. Her head rolled from side to side and her thighs trembled. "Look at me, Persephone!"

The blindfold was gone and she blinked at him in the dimness. His eyes glowed with a deep, orange fire, his body rising above her like a tower of heat. She touched her hands to the hardness of his belly, feeling the muscles working there as they rocked. He leaned over her, the weight of him leaving her happily breathless, his hips digging the clamp into her omi. She ran her hands over his upper arms, thick ropes of muscle bulging as he held himself above her. Their eyes locked and she felt herself trembling in response.

"Please, Aidon…" Her voice felt too soft in her throat, her body impossibly small beneath him. His stiff length throbbed between her legs, but he wasn't moving anymore. His eyes searched hers in the dimness. He knew just what she was asking for, but he held still, watching her, letting her beg. "Please."

"Tell me."

She had already said it. Her body said it with every breathless, quivering wave of pleasure. Why did the words stick so hard in her throat? Who was he—the Lord of Darkness, the great God of the Underworld? Was this the man who had taken her and slowly made her his with generous waves of pleasure and pain? She didn't know him—she didn't even know herself. She was lost, floating, gone. There was nothing left to give. She was already given.

She lifted her chin and swallowed. Her mouth trembled as she looked at his mouth and then back to his eyes. "Aidon…please…I want…"

He knew. She saw on his face he knew as he shifted, teasing her sex with the slick heat of his erection, slowly moving in and then back out. His eyes never left hers, watching her expression, as if reading her. As if he knew her.

"Tell me what I want to hear."

She squirmed beneath him, biting her lip. The heated flush in her cheeks spread down over her chest, through her belly, and seemed to radiate outward from her sex in waves. *I can tell him what he wants to hear.* She thought she would do anything to end this exquisite torture. Her fingernails dug into his arms and she lifted her sex to his, rolling her hips, dancing against his pelvis.

"I'm yours, Aidon." When her mouth opened to speak the words, she knew it was the truth. She raked her nails down over his arms and bucked up against him. "Take me!"

He groaned, sinking himself back into her, his hips pounding, his mouth crushing hers. Catching her wrists in one hand, he put them above her head as he slammed into her, the friction building between their thighs. She moaned and wrapped her legs around his waist, feeling her climax coming and working for it.

"Aidon!" She panted his name into his ear as she clutched him. He seemed to know she was close and lowered his head to her breast, his tongue flicking quickly over her swollen nipple. The sensation made her whimper, and when he bit the clamp and gently pulled it off, she screamed out loud, her sex beginning to spasm with pleasure. He quickly dipped his head to her other breast, skillfully removing the other with his teeth as her peak rose to impossible, shuddering heights. She struggled against him, against her orgasm, against the incredible sensation pulsing between her legs, but she was helpless to all of it.

And it didn't stop there. He continued to press into her, kneeling up and working his hard length between her thighs. The attachment over her omi throbbed with her fading climax, making her feel ready to burst. His fingers touched it and her eyes flew open wide. She had time to shake her head, but that was all. Aidon deftly slipped the clamp off, and like a dam bursting, the pressure building there now suddenly had somewhere to flow.

"Let it come again." He rubbed her tender flesh, round and round, and he sent her over the edge. She went without a thought, closing her eyes and sailing away under the slick friction of his fingers, the throbbing heat of his erection moving inside of her tight passage. Her hands reached for him, pulling him down to her, wanting to feel the weight of him as her whole body quivered with pleasure.

He gasped as the pulse and flutter of her sex spasmed around him. When she sank her teeth into his shoulder, he let out a low groan, his thighs pressing hers wide as he shoved as deep into her as he could go. It was a white-hot flood inside of her, and she whimpered, squeezing him harder, making him moan and buck against her. He whispered her name over and over in time with his thrusts until he was completely spent, panting in her ear.

When he went to roll off of her, she clung to him, turning them on their sides, belly to wet belly. His fingers brushed stray hair from her cheek, his eyes moving down her flushed breasts and belly, and then back up, meeting her eyes. She didn't understand the feeling filling her chest. It felt as if she might burst with something even more intense than her climax as they rested and watched each other in the silence.

"I—" The words caught in her throat, tripping over her lips. She swallowed hard, looking down at the bed, the dark bedclothes trapped at the edge, the golden balls, still humming their song, resting on the mattress. The nipple clamps shifted underneath her, digging into her side, and she saw the blindfold he had used to keep her in darkness. There was the paddle he had spanked her with, and yes, a riding crop, and the long plume of a feather. Her body buzzed with the memory—it had known, long before her head—she belonged to him.

As if listening to her thoughts, Aidon smiled, tracing his fingertip down her upper arm. "The first thing I will do is mark you as my own."

"Mark me?" She lifted her wide eyes to his, a hot flash of fear stabbing her belly.

He rolled off the bed, standing and holding his hand out to her. "Come with me."

Chapter Six

"What is this place?" Persephone drew close to Aidon's side as they walked together into a large, dimly lit room. "Are these mortals?"

"Not for long." Aidon nodded toward where Tisi stood, with the scourge tipped with scorpions he had told her of, whipping the skin off the back of a screaming man. "They are being punished. Most will die here."

"And who are they?" She pointed toward a small creature pacing behind Tisi. It was clearly a woman, or something with the vague shape of a woman, with dark eyes and long raven-colored hair. Still, the thing only came up to Persephone's waist, and there was something about the arms…

"The Keres." Aidon reached down and patted one of them on the head. Persephone hadn't even noticed, but there were many of them. This one had coiled its thick, snake-like arms around his knees three times. "Not now, Pet."

"Pet?" Persephone raised her eyebrows at the endearment.

Aidon mirrored her expression and then smiled. "Her name is Petulantia…it means *wantonness*."

"I can see that." Persephone watched as the Ker reluctantly unwrapped her arms and slid away.

"There are many Keres." Aidon pointed to the one behind Tisi. "That is Discordia, there. And behind her is Miseria. They are all sisters." Miseria had tears running down her cheeks, and Persephone would later come discover this was a constant thing with her. Discordia was the one pacing back and forth, occasionally licking her lips when the man Tisi was beating gave a particularly loud wail.

"They are the servants of the Underworld." Aidon patted a long table with drawers underneath and looked at her. "Sit here."

"Up there?" Her eyes moved over the instruments at the end of the table, sharp objects in strange shapes.

"I do not mind your questions." He placed his hands on her hips, lifting her easily and setting her down hard on the cold surface. She gasped, her surprised eyes meeting his. "But if you are to be mine, you will learn to obey when I tell you to do something." Frowning, she opened her mouth to speak, but his fingers pressed her lips. "The only thing I want to hear you say is 'Yes, Aidon.'"

Swallowing the words in her throat, she nodded. "Yes, Aidon."

"Good." He nodded his approval. "Lie down."

"Yes, Aidon." She swung her legs up onto the table and leaned back on her elbows. Looking up as she settled herself onto the cold surface, she saw her response had pleased him.

"Okay, Pet..." Aidon's hand reached down and patted the Ker who had wrapped herself around his thighs again. "I need you to do something for me."

"Anything, Master." Her voice was full of longing, and Persephone was suddenly glad she couldn't see what the Ker was doing down there.

"I need you to brand my queen." Aidon smiled down at Persephone, his finger moving over her upper arm. "One here." He touched her other arm. "Another here."

"Brand?" Persephone squeaked. "You don't mean...what I think you mean?"

The Ker was already using her strong arms to boost herself up onto the table next to Persephone. Before she knew what was happening, those arms had coiled themselves around her body, pinning her own arms down next to her sides. Petulantia was clearly made of flesh, although the way her limbs moved and stretched seemed impossible.

"Which one, Master?" Petulantia held up several strips of metal twisted into strange patterns.

"Aidon!" Persephone's voice was breathy as the Ker squeezed her chest, forcing the air from her lungs. "Please! Don't!'

He pressed his fingers to her lips, shaking his head. "What do I want to hear?"

Persephone pleaded with her eyes. "Please...Aidon...you don't mean to burn me...to brand me...the pain alone!"

"Trust me." He covered her mouth completely with his big hand. She opened her mouth to tell him she couldn't—how could she trust a man who had kidnapped her, beaten her, taken her virginity? Then she met his eyes, and saw no malice there, no ill-intent.

When she nodded, he took his hand away. "Yes, Aidon."

Smiling, he leaned down and kissed her forehead. "It will only hurt for a moment. I have a salve from Hypnos that puts the pain to sleep almost instantly."

"Master?" Petulantia, her arms wrapped around Persephone's upper body at least three times, still had her hands free, and in them she held those twisted metal shapes. "Which?"

"This." Aidon produced another metal shape from the drawer under the table, holding it up:

άδησ

It was his name, and she was to wear it for all to see, branded on both arms. Persephone thought of her mother, what Demeter would say, and closed her eyes against it. What choice did she have? She was here, in the Underworld, with no way out, and she knew Aidon meant to keep her. His reputation for never letting anyone out of the Realm of the Dead was beyond legendary.

"I need hot coals, Master." Petulantia nodded toward the fire burning in the hearth. Persephone watched as Aidon retrieved them from the fire in a small metal bin with a wooden handle. She could smell the smoke and she turned her head to the wall away from it. Petulantia's voice was soft in her ear. "I will do them quickly."

Persephone moaned softly, shaking her head, refusing to open her eyes. The Ker's grip tightened around her chest until she felt as if she had no breath at all left. She smelled it first, the hot singe of flesh, and then the fire raced through her upper arm, all the way up into her shoulder. She screamed, gritting and gnashing her teeth as the other arm was burned as well, the hot smell of her own flesh making her stomach turn.

She couldn't help looking as Petulantia rubbed something into her skin. It was black and sank into the wound as if her flesh were soil soaking up water. The pain was like a hot glow, a blooming fire in her chest.

"It hurts," she gasped, wincing as the Ker rubbed harder. Persephone looked at Petulantia's hands, now stained with black, and blistered and burned from the fire. "Your hands!"

"Do not worry." The Ker shook her head. "We feel little pain, and our limbs are regenerative."

Then, Aidon's hands moved on her, his fingers taking over where Petulantia had been massaging as the Ker uncoiled herself. "This should help." His big hands rubbed her upper arms, and almost instantly, the pain disappeared.

"It's gone." Persephone looked up at him in wonder. "It doesn't hurt at all!"

He smiled his approval, using a cloth to wipe his hands clean. "Don't move." His voice halted her motion and she gave him a questioning look. He turned to the Ker, who had slid down off the table. "Thank you, Pet. I think Tisi is just about done, if you want to go join the fun."

"Fun?" Persephone strained her neck to see, watching the scene at a strange angle. The man hanging limp from the restraints was bloody and broken. His open eyes began to glaze over. Tisi gave an enormous shriek of disappointment as the mortal's soul rose from his battered body. The apparition's resemblance to his human form was remarkable, and he gave Tisi a terrified look before sailing toward the door.

"He's ours!" Discordia leapt on the corpse, her arms wrapping around it, and Persephone saw, for the first time, the retractable claws of the Ker that tore into the flayed human flesh. Miseria and Petulantia fell onto the body as well, and the wet sound of them tearing the man apart made Persephone cringe and look away.

"They eat humans?" Persephone looked at Aidon, her eyes filled with horror.

Aidon shrugged. "It's what they do. When they're not here, they're usually hanging around battlefields, waiting for men to die so they can devour their bodies."

"What did that man do to deserve such a death?" Persephone watched as Tisi spread her wings and shook them free of the mortal's blood.

"Tisi has a thing about family killing family." Aidon reached under the table and set a wooden box next to Persephone. "That one…I believe he drowned his newborn daughter."

She stared at him, her mouth agape. "Mortals!"

"Tell me about it." Tisi had snuck up on them both and Persephone jumped at the sound of her voice. The snakes that coiled around her head like hair hissed as the Fury leaned over to look at the blonde goddess stretched out on the table. "Apparently, that was his fourth child, and he desperately wanted a son. Or at least, that was his excuse when he was begging for his life."

"Tisi…" Aidon sighed.

The Fury cocked her head, looking at Persephone's arm. "Nice. Branded and everything, huh? Does it hurt?"

She shook her head. "Aidon gave me something…"

"Hypnos' pain-sleep," he explained, giving Tisi a sidelong look. "I know you don't have much use for it."

Tisi laughed, the sound like breaking crystal. "When I use a brand, I want it to burn."

"I'm aware." Aidon shook his head. "Can you do me a favor, Tis?" The Fury waited, crossing her arms. Her hands and claws still showed blood, Persephone noticed with a little shudder. "Can you keep everyone out of the inner chamber? Sephie and I...we're going to be in my room for a few days."

"Days?" Tisi grinned and laughed when Aidon gave her a quelling look. "Will do. Have fun!" She gave them a quick wave and winked at Persephone. "Nice to see you again."

Persephone raised her hand in a polite wave and almost laughed to herself at the ridiculousness of the gesture. Who observed any rules of decency here, where monsters lived and mortals were flayed and devoured?

"I have something for you." Aidon opened the intricately carved wooden box. He held up a soft leather strap with two silver loops on each end. The same writing άδησ was branded into the leather on each side. Slipping it around her neck, he took a silver lock from the box and hooked it through each loop. Locking the collar in place with a small key, he put the key back into the box. "This shows everyone who you belong to."

"These weren't enough?" She gave him a rueful smile, glancing down at the wounds on her arms.

His smile had an edge to it. "Some day, you will cherish those marks, and I'd wager you will even ask for more."

Persephone gave a doubtful laugh. "If you say so."

His finger traced circles over her hip. "Would you like a bath?"

She didn't trust her voice, so she just nodded. He stood, holding his hand out, and she took it, letting him help her up.

* * * *

Leading her into the outer chamber of his rooms, he pointed toward the corner opposite the bubbling spring. A mirrored vanity stood there, the top full of lotions and creams. She opened the top drawer and discovered all sorts of bejeweled hair clips and ties. He looked at her for a moment, bemused. "I had something prepared for you."

"This was all planned for me?" She frowned. "When did you do this?"

"I've known for some time you would be mine." His eyes followed her movements as she began to put her hair up on top of her head. "I did ask your father for your hand, Persephone."

Her eyes widened. "You talked to Zeus?"

"He gave you to me." He smiled, a rare thing, not without a wicked sort of gleam. "It was just a matter of timing, after that."

"So you and my absent father made all the arrangements?" She spoke with a hairclip clamped between her teeth. "What about me?"

"You?" He shrugged. "You were the prize. You don't consult the boar when you send the dogs out to hunt it."

"Now I'm a boar?" She rolled her eyes, placing the last clip and dropping her hands to her sides.

Aidon frowned. "No. I—"

"I'm the Goddess of Spring, remember?" Her hands went to her hips and she glared at him. "Someone could have consulted me! I'm not a child, and I'm certainly not a piece of property to be given away!"

He slipped behind her, taking both her hands and putting them behind her back, clasping them there. He could hold her wrists with one hand and he did, sliding his other hand around her front to cup her breast.

"I'm not…" Her voice trailed off as he rolled her nipple between his thumb and finger. "Oh…don't…"

"What were you saying?" His mouth sought out the now bared skin of her neck, sucking at the tender flesh there.

She snarled at him like something wild and feral. His grip tightened too hard for her to break free. "I'm not an animal—some boar—to be hunted!"

"You seemed to enjoy the hunt," he commented as he nibbled her shoulder. "The struggle…"

She growled at him in frustration, twisting in his arms. He let her go with a chuckle, watching her as she stalked across the room toward the bubbling hot spring.

"Go away!" She glared at him over her shoulder and this time he laughed out loud, the sound reverberating against the rocky walls.

Persephone ignored him, sinking into the pool and marveling at the smoothness of the walls. The edges were rocky crags, but below her feet, the stone was smooth. She wondered idly where the water came from, and warm steam rose around her as she sank into the depths up to her shoulders with a soft groan.

A boar! Indignation filled her chest and she opened one eye, seeing him gone. She ignored the little twinge of disappointment in her belly and leaned back, enjoying the softly bubbling water of the spring all over her aching body. Her bottom still felt raw and sore from Aidon's attention.

She realized this was the first time she had really been truly alone since the abduction. Thoughts of her mother came to her mind. How worried she would be! What would Demeter say about what she and Aidon had done together? Persephone couldn't deny she had allowed it. He had given her the chance to leave, and she had chosen to stay. To be beaten. To be bound. To be branded. She glanced down at the dark marks on each of her upper arms. His name, carved into her skin. Yet there was, strangely, still no hint of pain.

Her face flushed at the thought of Demeter discovering the name of her lover permanently tattooed on her flesh. *Aidon's wrath is nothing compared to my mother's*, Persephone thought with a shudder. Staying here didn't seem like such a bad idea, considering the furious storm that waited for her at home.

And there was Aidon...

She found herself remembering the man who had once caught her attention chopping wood in the forest, how her body had responded to just the sight of him. But that was nothing, she discovered, compared to the reaction of her body to the god who had just taken her to his bed. No one had ever opened her up the way he did. He stripped her down bare, beyond naked, and made her do things she never thought she could.

Careful what you wish for. Artemis' words echoed in her head. She had longed for something more. She had even spoken of Elysium! Had some part of her really longed for this? The memory of Aidon's hands, his mouth, his eyes, all made her breathless and too-warm in the steaming pool. No one had ever dared to touch her that way, to push her to such limits, to force her to swallow her strong-willed pride and humble herself like he had.

She knew what Artemis and Athena would say—and what her mother would say. She knew they would all be aghast at her kneeling before and submitting to a man, no matter what kind of god he was. Yet she had felt so much power in her submission, so much freedom in her humiliation. She didn't understand the paradox, but she knew how it made her feel. He made her feel like she could fly.

And he did, somehow, seem to know her already. It was as if he could sense her wishes before she even spoke them out loud. How that was possible, she didn't know, but she had seen and heard stranger things here in the Underworld, and she didn't doubt it was true. It felt true.

Glancing at the open door, she wondered where he had gone. Had she really offended him, when she told him to go away? The thought of hurting his feelings seemed impossible, but she sensed a big heart beating in that huge chest of his. Almost as if to prove her point, Aidon came into the room, closing the door softly behind him.

Persephone closed her eyes, pretending not to notice, but her pulse began to quicken just feeling his presence. The silence grew long and she sighed, shifting in the pool. Finally, she couldn't stand it any longer and she opened her eyes, looking for him. He sat in a chair in the corner, just watching her. His face lingered in shadow, and she wanted to know what he might be thinking.

"I thought you'd gone."

He leaned forward, clasping his hands between his knees. "You can't get rid of me that easily, Sephie." She smiled in spite of herself, lifting her hand and flicking water toward him. He was much too far away to reach, but he stood, walking toward the pool. "Besides, I thought you might need some time to be alone."

Can he read my mind? She looked up at him standing at the edge of the pool, her eyes moving up his thick, strong calves and thighs, his hard, flat stomach, and his strong, broad chest. This was no woodcutter. This was a god among men, and he had the finest form she had ever seen. The easy power and grace of his body, the quiet, subtle strength of his movements, completely transfixed her gaze.

He held his hand out to her, as if he wanted her to stand. She could see her own reflection in the vanity mirror behind him as she stood, water mixed with the bubbles from the spring slipping down her skin. She had gathered her hair up, but tendrils fell down in the steam, making soft blonde curls against her shoulders. She loved the way he looked at her body, like he wanted to keep her.

The cool air hardened her still swollen nipples almost immediately. Aidon pointed toward the ceiling and twirled his finger, silently asking her to turn around. He eased into the water behind her, his hands roaming over her wet skin before reaching for a soft, folded cloth on the edge of the pool. In his hand, he had a sweet-smelling bar of soap. She watched him in the reflection of the mirror as he began to bathe her, his eyes following the path the cloth took, over her shoulders and down her back. His touch was tender, almost reverent.

"I first saw you at Demeter's harvest." He kissed her shoulder before soaping it, careful of her upper arm, where the brand was still raw. "Does it hurt here?"

Persephone shook her head. "No. Hypnos' pain-sleep seems to work long."

"He can work wonders." Aidon slipped the sudsy cloth down her arm, catching her hand in his. "I asked him to make me a love-sleep, soon after that day I saw you wandering in the meadow."

"A love-sleep?" She watched as he pressed his palm to hers. Her fingers were dainty and slim next to his. "Is there such a thing?"

Aidon sighed. "Apparently not." He raised her hand above her head, and then raised the other, holding them there by the wrists as he slid the cloth down each slender arm. "I had hoped there might be…something. Because after that day, I could think of little else but you." He pressed his body to hers as he soaped up her breasts, watching in the mirror as the cloth circled her nipples.

"Why me?"

He slid the cloth over the soft, smooth skin of her belly, dipping briefly into her navel. For a moment, she thought he wasn't going to respond, but then he dropped her arms, stepping back to meet her eyes in the mirror as they fell to her side.

"You were crying." His finger reached out to twirl a soft ringlet of her hair. "I had come up only for a moment, at Hecate's request. There was…oh never mind, that's not important." He gave her a rueful smile, still twisting her hair around his finger. "I saw you, alone, walking through the field, with flowers springing up and blooming in your wake…but you had these fat tears running down your cheeks…"

Persephone tried to remember when it might have been, what she could have been sad about, but couldn't recall. She had attended her mother's harvests since she was old enough to walk, and they all ran together in her mind.

"Believe me when I tell you I have seen great beauty in my time, goddess." His eyes met hers in the mirror and her breath caught at the expression there. "But I had never seen such beautiful pain. I knew, then, I had found a woman whose heart's depths were vast enough to understand the darkness here…" She saw him swallow before he continued.

"The darkness in me…" His finger traced his own name branded on her arm. "The darkness hidden in you…"

"Why did you not ask my mother for me that day?"

Her inquiry startled him and he frowned. "Well, for one thing, I know your mother." He shook his head and snorted. "She would have taken after me with a scythe." Persephone couldn't help smiling. He was probably right. "And I thought…perhaps…given time…I might forget about those beautiful tears…" He moved the cloth lightly over her back, busying himself with the task at hand, his eyes refusing to meet hers again. He caressed her gently when he came to her bottom, still pink from her spanking.

Persephone couldn't stop herself. "Did you want to forget?"

"No." Aidon almost smiled at her question as he slid the soapy cloth over her hip. "But I tried. For your sake."

"Mine?" She turned to face him, looking up to meet his eyes. There was a sadness there she didn't understand.

"This…" He waved his hand, glancing toward the door with a sigh. "This place. There are few who can look past the outer appearances and appreciate what beauty lies here."

"But you thought…that I might?"

He nodded. "I knew you would."

"Yet you hesitated to bring me here?" She stepped toward him, the bubbling water swirling around her thighs as the steam rose between them.

"I didn't know if the God of the Underworld would be much of a prize to one such as you," he admitted with a frown. "Perhaps I felt it would be a bit…one-sided."

Persephone slipped her arms around his waist and rested her head against his chest. She heard his heart beating, feeling it against her flushed cheek. Her words were soft, unwavering, and she remembered with sudden surprise what she had been sad about that day.

"I dreamed of you." She smiled when his arms went around her and he stroked her hair as he listened. "That day you saw me crying. That was the day I told my mother about a dark man in a chariot with dark horses, who would one day come and take me to be his Queen…" His body stiffened against hers in surprise. "Do you know what she said?"

"Hmm?"

"That it was the worst nightmare she had ever heard." Persephone winced at the memory. It had been harvest time, just a year ago, when she had gleefully told her mother of her dream of the dark stranger with his dark purpose. Demeter's face had gone white, her hands trembling at her throat as her daughter gushed on and on about the darkness that would someday come and claim her.

Aidon chuckled. "I am Demeter's worst nightmare."

"But not mine." She lifted her face to his, asking to be kissed with only her eyes. "You were my dream, not my nightmare."

His lips met hers in response, capturing her mouth as he crushed her to him. She gave him everything in that kiss. Every denial, even pent-up breath, every "no!" she had spoken, they all dissolved as she melted into his arms and let herself be carried away on a swift river of emotion. When the kiss broke, he looked at her hopefully, his eyes filled with longing. She tried to reassure him silently because she couldn't find the words.

Aidon took a deep breath. "I keep what I love." His fingers briefly touched her cheek. "But I do love what I keep."

He didn't let her respond. Instead, he turned her around again to face the mirror. A gentle pressure against her back from his hand bent her over so she hung onto the other edge of the pool. He spread her thighs and tilted her bottom up. She imagined his eyes as they stared between her legs at the sparse blonde curls covering her swollen lips.

He lifted the cloth again and began to wash her, gently parting her sex and moving the material between. She sighed and moved her hips, arching to give him better access. He bathed her thighs, spreading them wider as he went. She looked at herself in the mirror, bent over for him, meeting her own eyes. No innocent young girl looked out at her anymore. The leather collar around her neck, the black tattoos on her upper arms, even her long, flowing hair piled high on top of her head, all made her different somehow.

She gasped when Aidon filled a silver goblet with water and began to rinse her, letting the warmth run over her skin in rivulets. Again and again, he poured the hot liquid over her behind, letting it drip down over her sex. Then his fingers traced the same path, down the line of her spine and the crack of her behind, delving into her sex. She met his eyes in the mirror and saw his erection rising behind her, throbbing with his pulse, and she knew what he wanted.

He knelt down beside her in the pool, his tongue making circles over the back of her thigh. One hand went to cup her breast and she moaned, arching against his mouth, suddenly aching to feel his hardness inside of her. He seemed to be able to touch her everywhere at once, and the shift and weight of him moved like bright heat behind her as he began to worship every inch of her slick, soapy body with his mouth and his hands.

"Aidon," she murmured, reaching behind for him and grasping his hair. She pressed his face between her legs and he groaned, his tongue lost in her soft folds. She couldn't seem to get enough of him, and somehow he knew it. "Oh please, don't tease me. I want to feel you inside of me."

Aidon stood, grabbing her hips and pressing forward into her, filling her to bursting. She moaned, raking her nails across the rough edge of the pool. The water sloshed as they began to rock, and she felt the slap of his belly as he thrust, deeper and deeper, trying to bury himself in her depths.

She gripped the edge, for balance, meeting his thrusts with her own, pumping back against him and spreading even wider. She loved the way he grabbed her hips, using them to push in harder. He leaned into her, one of his hands cupping a wet, swaying breast, the other reaching around and between her legs to rub her wet, aching sex. He forced her onward, upward, impaling her with every delicious inch of him as the friction built between them.

The high water rose in swells and waves with their motion, spattering the mirrored surface behind the pool. Persephone reached back with one hand, grabbing his thigh and pulling him in deeper, making him moan and shove her forward. The water sloshed right over the side with that push. She tried to adjust herself for balance as he suddenly pulled out of her, going down to his knees behind her. His hands steadied her, pulling her with him, back into him, using her hips to tug her. With both of them in the pool, the water began to spill over the sides in a steady flood, the steam rising around them.

She rocked back into him, impaling herself again and again. Slipping her hand under the water, she rubbed herself until her fingers were wrinkled and her sex throbbed for release.

"Aidon...Aidon..." She called his name over and over, feeling him reach around and pull her belly, using the leverage to meet her as she ground her hips into him, dancing back on his iron rod. She forgot about the water sloshing out around them. She forgot about everything but the white hot sensation.

She begged him for release, knowing it remained up to him, but she didn't know how. Aidon groaned, low and loud, and pushed her quickly off of him. He grabbed her and turned her around to him, slipping back up into her without any guidance or direction at all. She noticed half of the water gone, all over the black stone floor, but saw it only peripherally. She worked her sex down onto him, his hands grabbing her hips. When she bit at his shoulder, he growled, urging her to arch backward as he nuzzled her breasts. He sucked and nipped at them, making her squeal and squirm in his lap.

He panted her name, his breath coming faster. She felt his cock beginning to swell inside of her as she looked at his face. What she saw there sent her right over a rocking, slick edge, arching and falling into the glowing darkness of his eyes as she began to climax, too. His length pulsed between her thighs, spilling endless heat in long, shuddering waves.

They rocked together still in the wet warmth as she wrapped herself around him completely, not wanting to let go. Now half the water had flooded the floor. The air had grown cool and she snuggled closer, trying to get warmer.

"Cold?" He kissed her ear. She nodded and he stood, taking her with him. He carried her out of the pool, across the wet floor, and opened a cupboard. He threw several bath sheets on the floor to soak up the water and then let her down, wrapping one around her and rubbing her slowly dry. They didn't speak, but their eyes met several times, and spoke volumes. When they were both dry, he pulled her close, breathing deep as he began to take the pins out of her hair.

"I'm hungry," she murmured against his chest, letting him free her tresses. They fell down her back in soft waves.

She heard his smile. "The queen makes demands!"

It startled her to hear him speak of her that way, and she wondered about her newly acquired role as Aidon led her back into the bedroom. Everything had been cleaned up and put away, the bed made. Even the bowl he had knocked to the floor rested back in its place on the night table, full to the brim with fruit. She climbed up onto the bed and stretched her limbs, feeling very much like a queen, and smiling as he fetched a pomegranate from the bowl of fresh fruit on the bedside table. He broke it open with his thumbs, revealing the fleshy seeds inside. She smelled the ripeness of it, a sweet tang.

"Do you really want to stay with me?" His eyes met hers only for a moment as his fingers dipped into the fleshy middle of the fruit. "Do you want to accept your place as Queen of the Underworld?"

"Yes." Persephone nodded, giving him a smile. "I do."

"You will be free here, Sephie. You can go where you will. This is your home now." Aidon cleared his throat, his eyes downcast. "The only concession is you can never leave the Underworld."

"Never?"

"You are not a twain-traveler." He shrugged. "Perhaps, after we are married..."

"Married?" Her eyes widened at the thought of a wedding in the Underworld.

He dug his fingers into the red, ripe fruit in his hand. "I would not keep you as a concubine. You will be my wife." She recognized it as a proposal and command all at once. He lifted his fingers to show her the juicy fruit. "Are you sure, Persephone? Anyone who eats anything in the Underworld must stay here. It's the law."

She nodded, pulling his cupped hand, full of fruit, toward her mouth. It dripped over her belly and breasts, leaving a sticky seed trail. She spoke the words he had taught her, the ones he wanted to hear. "Yes, Aidon." She sucked the fleshy red fruit off his fingers, crunching the bittersweet seeds.

He watched her lick his hand, cleaning off the juices, his eyes smiling. Her tongue lapped between his fingers and over his palm as he dipped his head toward her middle, cleaning the syrupy red mess from her belly with his mouth. Persephone moaned when he found a stray seed near her nipple, her mouth sucking furiously at his finger. She forgot all about her hunger, just as she had forgotten about the deep, red sting of her bottom, and she closed her eyes and let herself be carried away on a sticky red wave of bittersweet bliss.

Chapter Seven

Persephone noticed the new ebony throne first, sitting empty beside Aidon's. Her heart thrummed in her chest and she felt heat in her cheeks as she approached him. She noticed his eyes glowed as he watched her. She had massed her golden hair up high on top of her head and adorned it with the glitter of diamonds and other jewels. She wore nothing except for a long black veil fastened amidst the jewelry in her hair. The veil pulled back from her face and hung down her back in lacy layers that seemed to make her skin glow even brighter with a pale light. Her skin, adorned with another, curvy brand along the small of her back, and another just above her sex, glowed with a golden dust applied with a soft bristled brush. Aidon had been right about that. She cherished every mark of his on her body.

The cavern walls were dark as night, but the ghostly light of the cypress tree lit the guests' faces. The shades were too numerous to count. They had all stopped in the process of being judged, or bathing in the Pool of Lethe, to watch this event. Tisi stood to the side with her sisters, Megaera and Alecto, and in front of them, Thanatos, and his brother, Hypnos. The Moirai giggled together as she passed and Persephone glanced at them. The three Fates never separated, and their beady eyes missed nothing. Of course, there stood dear Hecate, fading in and out next to them, as she was wont to do when she became nervous.

Aidon held his hand out to her and Persephone took a deep breath as she stepped toward him. She now knew he was her destiny, and nothing could keep her from it. His gaze swept over her form as she stood before him. On the smaller thrones to the right sat the three judges of the shades, their eyes on her as well. She had grown used to her constant state of undress, and their gaze didn't bother her.

"Kneel." Aidon squeezed her hand and Persephone sank to her knees before him, bowing her golden head, the black veil brushing her pink cheeks. "Persephone, Goddess of Spring and all things bright and golden…will you consent to be my bride, to rule beside me as Queen of the Underworld, for all of eternity?"

"Yes." The word passed over her lips with barely enough breath to carry it, but somehow they all heard her assent. A cheer went up, filling the cavern with sound. She felt her blush as Aidon lifted her chin, his eyes searching hers. He seemed satisfied with what he found there because he smiled, his whole face brightening with the gesture.

"Forever more, you will belong to me." Aidon lifted a small, intricately carved wooden box. When he opened it to reveal the contents, a collective gasp went up through the room. Persephone, however, couldn't speak. She could barely even breathe. The necklace was the most beautiful thing she had ever seen. Each of the silver links of the delicate chain seemed to sparkle in the light, and at the center rested a large red ruby surrounded by diamonds whose weight seemed too heavy for the chain to bear.

"Hephaestus made this for me." Aidon's voice lowered, meant only for her, as he leaned in to fasten it around her neck. "It will feel as if you are wearing nothing, but will never come off. You are bound to me forever, Persephone. You are mine."

Aidon unlocked the fading leather collar around her neck, the one with his name branded in the side, and set it aside. She gasped as the new chain tightened around her neck and then went slack. Sure it had dropped to the ground, she panicked, reaching for it. With a sigh of relief, she felt it, the ruby resting at the center of her throat, beating with the heat of her pulse there. The chain encircled her neck and even at the back, she felt no fastener or clasp. It had simply become a part of her.

When she looked up at him in wonder, he smiled again, and reached out to trace the line of her jaw with his finger. It was a tender moment, an intimate sharing in the midst of the crowd, and the way he looked at her made her glad she knelt instead of stood. She knew her legs might not have held her otherwise. In that moment, she could think of nothing more than the time they had spent, days and days, locked in his room, ignoring the calls on the other side of the door.

When Aidon produced a pomegranate, breaking the flesh open between them, Persephone's memory triggered again, and she flushed. They had shared this very fruit together on their first night. Aidon had licked and sucked the seeds from her navel…and her…

"Eat." The sticky bittersweet juices dripped down over his hands as he held the fruit out to her. Everyone who resided in the Underworld knew what this ritual meant. Anyone who ate the food of the dead, food grown in the Underworld, would reside forever in the land of the dead.

Persephone leaned in and, using her tongue as a spoon, scooped the flesh of the fruit, sucking it into her mouth. Aidon watched as she chewed the bittersweet seeds, swallowing and licking the red juice from her lips. When he set the fruit aside, she grasped his hands, using her tongue to clean them of pomegranate juice. She licked his palm, the inside of his wrist, and even wiggled her tongue between the grooves of his fingers.

"Persephone…" His voice sounded pained, barely above a whisper as he she sucked one of his fingers deep into her mouth. She saw the gentle rise of his erection underneath the dark loincloth he wore and thrilled at it, sucking harder at his finger. "Not now…"

"But I'm hungry now," she murmured, tracing her tongue over the pads of his fingers and then dropping her mouth to his thigh where a splotch of red fruit had stuck. She sucked it off the skin there, licking circles, making him gasp.

"You are so very, very bad." Aidon lifted her chin and saw the mischievous smile playing over her lips. "Careful, you might make me believe you want to be punished." His gaze traveled over her body. "Stand." His voice rose loud enough for the others to hear, and she stood with his help. He towered over her as he stood as well, grasping her hand

and announcing, "I give you Persephone, Queen of the Underworld!"

The applause shook the cavern. Even the muted sounds of the shades, cheering in the strange language of the dead, seemed festive as they all clamored forward to meet their new Queen. She expected the dark throne to be cold, but looked up at Aidon in surprise at the warmth under her bottom as she sat beside him. The ebony throne seemed to conform to her body temperature, making her nude form comfortable, not too warm or too chilled.

"Hephaestus again," Aidon leaned in and said with a wink. "Besides, it's fitting, isn't it? We are in Hell, after all…"

Persephone took Tisi's outstretched hand, but smiled over at Aidon. "No, my love. This is Heaven."

"Glad to see you so happy." Tisi leaned in and kissed Persephone on the cheek as the three Furies gave their blessings and began to depart.

"Where are you off to?" Aidon caught Tisi's hand. "Stay, drink, eat. There's a delectable feast in the Great Hall!"

Tisi shook her head, the black snakes there hissing in unison. "I'm afraid we've got work to do. Souls to torture and maim…you know how it is." She waved her hand toward the other three judges sitting next to them who had resumed their duties. Shades came forward one at a time, lining up endlessly behind one another.

"It's true." Thanatos moved in behind Tisi, flashing his toothy smile. "There's no rest for the wicked."

"Hey." Tisi winked over her shoulder at him. "Do you mean me…or them?"

His grin widened and Persephone marveled at how many rows of teeth he seemed to have in there! "Wicked is as wicked does?"

Tisi sighed and put her hand to her forehead. "Then I am so going to Hell…oh, wait…" She winked at Aidon and

Persephone. "So, Thanatos, which wicked mortal's got your panties all in a bunch?"

For the first time, Persephone could see where the God of Death got his reputation. His eyes flashed and he bared his teeth—all of them—making her gasp and shrink against Aidon's side.

"Sisyphus!" Thanatos spat. "Didn't you hear?"

Tisi glanced over at her sisters, who nudged and tried to shush her, Persephone noticed. Tisi blinked innocently. "No…what happened, Thannie?"

"Tisi…" Aidon's warning tone came too late.

Thanatos was off and running. "First Zeus sends me after him, like the God of Death is now his personal lapdog or something!" Tisi rolled her eyes at that. Persephone had learned quite quickly Zeus wasn't a favorite among those who lived in the Underworld. "According to our self-appointed leader, I'm supposed to chain this Sisyphus down here and leave him to rot. Fair enough, nothing unusual so far, right?"

Tisi nodded and Persephone felt Aidon sigh. He looked between Tisi and Thanatos as if they were two small children he just knew were going to end up in a fight he would have to break up.

"Then the sneaky little mortal tricks me!" Thanatos snorted indignantly.

Tisi grinned. "A mere mortal tricked the God of Death? Thannie, you're losing your touch!"

He glared at the Fury. "You didn't hear him! He was incredibly cunning—I swear, Aidon, he could sell souls to the living!" Thanatos looked to Aidon for help, but the God of the Dead just shrugged.

"Oh come on!" Tisi laughed. "I still can't believe you fell for it! 'Oh, great God of Death, I don't understand how these chains work, can't you show me?' And you, ya muttonhead, snap the chains on yourself!" The Furies and the Fates all giggled now, and even Hecate went invisible to hide her own laughter.

"Okay, okay!" Thanatos held up his hand. "I know how it looks."

"What happened then?" Persephone asked. She remembered Thanatos mentioning Sisyphus when he hastened on his way to chain him up and tried to hide her smile.

"I stayed chained up in Tartarus for three days." Thanatos glowered at Aidon. "No thanks to you, I might add."

"Where were you?" Persephone nudged him.

Aidon gave her a dark look. "We were busy."

"Oh." Persephone flushed.

"So while you two were locked in your bedroom refusing to answer the door..." Tisi winked and went on. "Poor Thannie was locked in chains...until Ares came to save him."

"Ares?" Persephone inquired. "The God of War?"

Aidon sighed. "He apparently got tired of fighting losing battles."

Persephone looked between them, confused. "What does that—?"

"If I can't get topside, then no one can die," Thanatos explained. "So Ares was up there, hacking away, mortals' heads were rolling...but it didn't do him any good. He had headless bodies chasing bodiless heads, the wrong heads being put back on the wrong bodies, mix and match limbs..."

"Oh, no!" Persephone hid a smile behind her hand.

"Oh yes!" Thanatos sighed. "There were some surprised should-be widows welcoming home their should-be-dead warriors for a few days there. It was awful! A huge mess to clean up, believe me. But that damned Sisyphus finally got what was coming to him!"

"I hope you weren't too gentle," Tisi teased.

Thanatos bared his teeth at her. "Not likely. Fool me once..."

"Sisyphus is a piece of work," Aidon agreed. "Zeus has been complaining about him for years. He's always been a petty thief. Then he took his own brother's throne—tricked him out of it somehow."

"That isn't what pushed old Zeusie over the edge, though!" Tisi laughed, leaning in toward Persephone to murmur, "He told everyone about Zeus' escapades with Aegina. I think the whole heavens shook when Hera found out about that one!"

"Zeus cheated on his wife?" Persephone's eyes widened.

Thanatos raised his eyebrows. "Are you that innocent? Zeus has been cheating on Hera since the Titans set up shop in Tartarus."

"She gets all upset, but then does it right back to him," Tisi countered.

"Which may be something my brother tolerates," Aidon remarked. "But I will not."

"Nor I." Persephone frowned at him. The thought of Aidon with another woman made her crazy. It was hard enough to tolerate his clear familiarity with the Furies, although she hadn't had the courage to ask about his past yet.

"Well, we're off to play avenger!" Tisi winked at Aidon and Persephone as she gathered her sisters and they started off, arm in arm. "Only call us if you really need us!"

Aidon waved them off, shaking his head and calling, "Just don't leave any heads on my doorstep this time!"

Persephone half-smiled, trying to tell if he was serious or not, when Aidon turned his attention back to Thanatos. The God of Death still, apparently, had a few bones to pick about being left in the lurch while Aidon was holed up with his new bride.

"Persephone, may I speak with you?" Hecate appeared by her side, startling the blonde goddess and making her gasp and touch the ruby resting at her throat.

Hecate appeared as young and beautiful, her blue-black hair falling nearly to her knees around her completely nude form. Persephone had finally gotten used to all the feminine nudity in the Underworld. The men usually wore a loincloth, but the women wore nothing at all.

Hecate leaned in and whispered, "Can we go for a walk?"

"Just let me tell my husband." The words made her smile.

The God of Death spoke to Aidon in a heated whisper as Persephone approached, "My workload has increased tenfold—mortals are freezing to death in their beds! All the other gods are starting to notice, and you know if Zeus figures out what's going on—"

Persephone touched Aidon's arm. "Figures out what?"

"Nothing a beautiful bride should worry about on her wedding day." Aidon kissed her cheek, giving Thanatos a quelling look.

Persephone looked between them for a moment, frowning. Finally, she turned to Aidon. "Hecate wishes to speak to me. Shall I go with her?"

His eyes met the dark-haired goddess' gaze and he studied her for a moment, frowning. Then he gave Persephone a nod. "Don't go far."

She leaned in and kissed his cheek before taking Hecate's hand and walking with her between the pools of Mnemosyne and Lethe.

"Did Tisi ever find the two shades Aidon sent to Elysium?" Persephone asked as the two goddesses began the ascent up the steep staircase guarded by the three headed dog, Cerberus. He raised only one head as they approached, his tail thumping, a clear indication he knew them both. Persephone had grown fond of him and stopped to scratch him behind the ears as Aidon did.

"Meleager's uncles?" Hecate led Persephone up the last few steps and they walked along the banks of the river Styx as they spoke. Up here, the walls glowed a deep, dark orange. "No, thankfully. He'd be scattered in tiny pieces all across Greece by now if she had."

"Well, I'm glad you saved at least one young, impetuous hero." Persephone followed Hecate as she settled herself into Charon's skiff. The boat rocked with the weight of the goddesses as the boatman ferried them across.

"I shouldn't meddle, but Tisi...she can be so vicious." Hecate gave Persephone a hand out of the boat. They were now on the opposite shore, near the entrance of the Underworld.

"It's justice, of sorts, I suppose." Persephone took the goddess' hand again as they walked toward the gates. Persephone, so involved in their conversation, realized for the first time how far they had come from the Chamber of Judgment. She remembered Aidon's warning not to go far with a stab of fear.

"Hecate, perhaps we should go back?" Persephone stopped short of the gates and the dark-haired goddess glanced back at her.

"You know I am a twain-traveler." Hecate turned and grasped the blonde goddess' hands in hers. "I can take you home, Sephie. Is this something you wish?"

Shaking her head, Persephone backed slowly away, her eyes wide. "No...I don't want to go back."

"You don't miss your mother?" Hecate cocked her head, her eyes searching. "I have spoken to her, you know. She misses you a great deal."

"My mother?" Persephone looked to where Hecate pointed, past the gates of Hades, where the world she had always known still resided. She knew her mother must be worried sick, wondering what had happened to her, but she had tried to block out the thought. "What did she say?"

"She asked me if I had seen what manner of god or mortal had stolen her fair daughter away." Hecate sighed, her dark eyes filled with sadness. "She was very distraught."

Persephone felt the blood drain from her own face at the thought. She grabbed Hecate's arm. "What did you tell her?"

"I told her the truth, at the time." The dark-haired goddess clasped Persephone's hand again and squeezed it. "I had heard your voice, but had not seen who had taken you."

Relieved, Persephone glanced again toward the gates. "Please don't tell her, Hecate. She wouldn't understand."

"She loves you." Hecate caught Persephone's gaze with her own. "She does nothing now but wander alone, calling and searching for you. Won't you give her some answer?"

Persephone shook her head, hugging her arms and looking across the river. What answer could she give her mother? What could she possibly tell her?

"She spoke of a necklace she gave you," Hecate continued. "For protection. She couldn't understand how you could have been taken if you'd been wearing it."

"I wasn't," Persephone frowned. "I took it off, just before Aidon—" She touched her throat, where the ruby pulsed now. She had traded one necklace for another. Her mother would never understand. Persephone turned from the gates and pulled away, shaking her golden head. "I can't, Hecate. Please, just don't tell her where I am."

"I won't betray you," Hecate agreed with a sigh. "But I would ask you to reconsider…at least tell her you are safe."

"No." Persephone backed away, raising her hands in a warding off gesture. "She would never allow me to stay here…and I can't imagine my life anywhere else."

"You are a woman, now." Hecate frowned. "And Queen of the Underworld. Perhaps it's time you started acting as such?"

Persephone's face flushed and her jaw set as she stared at the other goddess. "You will not tell me what to do." Turning, she stormed away down the shore, heading back toward the ferry and leaving Hecate standing near the gates. The dark-haired goddess didn't follow her.

Chapter Eight

Pacing the shore, Persephone waited and watched as Charon's boat emptied of its passengers on the opposite side, willing him to hurry. She wanted to get back to Aidon as quickly as she could. Glancing over her shoulder, she saw Hecate no longer standing by the gates, and she hoped the goddess wouldn't betray her and tell Demeter her location— or her activity.

"She has gone, Queen Persephone…"

Persephone whirled in the direction of the voice addressing her, surprised to find a shade sitting behind her on a rock. She found herself startled by her own ability to understand him. He spoke the language of the dead, and yet she recognized the words. *What magic is this?*

"Pardon me for addressing you so, my Queen." The older man stood and bowed low before her. She realized there must have been some change in things when she accepted her position as Queen of the Underworld. Aidon could understand the language of the dead, and now she could as well. "I should have asked your permission first."

"No, please…" Persephone shook her head, frowning. She was used to a great deal of attention as a beautiful, young goddess, but this kind of reverence and formal greeting wasn't something she had ever experienced and it made her uncomfortable. "Rise and come across the river with me."

The man shook his head sadly and glanced longingly across the black river, where Charon began his way back. "I am afraid I cannot. My wife left me no coin with which to cross over."

Frowning, Persephone watched the man sit back on the rock, his chin in his hand. A great scar crossed his cheek, like a half-moon, only partially hidden by his fingers. "I'm so sorry…were you too poor?"

"Oh, no." The man sighed again, his eyes on the skiff as it skimmed slowly toward them. "She had the coin, but chose not to send it with me. In fact, she left my body naked and unburied in the middle of the town square."

Persephone gasped, her eyes widening. "Blasphemy! That is no way to treat the dead!"

The man nodded, his eyes brimming with tears he bravely blinked back. "Just so, oh fair and righteous Queen of the Underworld. I wish there was some way to repay her unkindness to me, but I am stuck here forever on this side of the Styx…"

Her heart went out to him as she watched Charon dock his skiff against the rocky shore and begin to collect coin from the shades clamoring to climb on board.

"I am Queen of the Underworld," she murmured, almost as if reminding herself. She glanced back at the man sitting on the rock. He looked so sad and forlorn as he watched the other shades climbing on board the little boat. "Is there any way I might help you in your plight?"

He brightened, his eyes gleaming. "Perhaps there is, oh generous one. If you would give me permission to return, just to ask my wife to amend her ways and give me a proper burial…?"

Persephone glanced toward the gates, remembering Hecate's plea. Perhaps she could get a message to her mother after all. "If I let you go, will you deliver a message up there for me?"

The man nodded eagerly. "Anything, goddess!"

"Go to Demeter—Goddess of the Harvest, do you know of her?"

"Of course."

Persephone frowned, thinking. "Tell her…her daughter is safe and well and happy and she need not worry. Can you do that?"

"Indeed!" He stood, grinning, rubbing his hands together. "Does this mean I can go back up?"

Nodding, she smiled at him, pleased to grant such a simple request. "It shall be so. Go, shade…and come back to us as soon as you are given a proper rest and have delivered my message."

"Thank you, goddess!" He leapt up and burst toward the gates so quickly she felt more than saw him pass. A sudden chill went through her and then he was simply gone, disappearing through the gates at the end of the cavern.

When she sat in the boat, crossing the river Styx, she began to think twice about what she had done. It had seemed like such a simple request to grant, her first as Queen of the Underworld, and yet perhaps she should have waited to ask Aidon...

Things were all so different and new here, and she knew it would take time for her to get used to it all. She stopped to scratch Cerberus behind each ear, making his back leg twitch uncontrollably, before making her way back to the Chamber of Judgment.

Aidon still sat on his throne beside the three judges, but she saw Thanatos had departed. When Aidon saw her, he smiled, using his two-pronged scepter to wave her toward him. Most of the time, she almost forgot she spent her time here completely nude, until his eyes found her again. The realization filled her with heat as she advanced, feeling her black bridal veil brushing her hips as she walked.

Using the pressure of his scepter on her shoulder to guide her, he pressed her to kneel before his throne. Then he cupped her chin, his eyes searching her face. "You were gone too long, beauty."

She turned and kissed his palm and then pressed it against her cheek. "Every moment away from you is too long."

Smiling, he held his hand out to her. "Come, my Queen."

Persephone took the throne beside his, marveling again at its warmth. From here, they could see the entire Chamber of Judgment with its seemingly constant influx of shades entering and leaving again toward their final destinies. She thought briefly of the man whose pardon she had granted and wondered if she should tell Aidon about him.

"Hecate didn't return with you?"

Persephone flushed, remembering Hecate's berating tone. "She had other things to attend to."

"Everyone seems busy, except us." Aidon leaned over to kiss the nape of her neck. "Maybe we should go lock ourselves in our room again."

Persephone smiled as his lips traveled over her shoulder. "But what about what happened to poor Thanatos while we were locked away? Your kingdom clearly needs its king…"

"And its queen." Aidon's hand slipped down to her lap, massaging her slim thigh.

"What, exactly, do you do down here, anyway?" She wiggled away from his roaming hands, turning to look toward the three thrones on her left where each of the Underworld judges sat.

Aidon grinned. "As little work as I can get away with and as much pleasure as possible."

She laughed. "I'm serious."

"So am I." He winked and took her hand, caressing her palm with his thumb. "I am not so different here than I am in our bedroom."

Persephone flushed, trying to ignore the electric sensation traveling down her arm from the pressure of his hand against hers. "What do you mean?"

"I am known for my fairness." He lifted her hand to his mouth, kissing her palm. "I may be stern…even cruel…" His teeth raked over the sensitive flesh of her wrist and she gasped. "I have even been called unmerciful." His eyes glowed as he saw her respond to his touch. "But I am always just."

"Aidon…" she whispered breathlessly as he nibbled his way up her inner arm.

"Yes, my queen?"

She wasn't used to being called that and it made her feel too small and too big all at once. Trying to change the subject, she asked, "You didn't answer my question. What exactly is it you do? Is it all about sitting on a throne all day?"

He chuckled, pulling gently at the tender skin at the inside of her elbow with his teeth. "Hardly. I forget how little time you have been in this world."

"It takes getting used to," she agreed, turning her eyes toward the ghostly light of the cypress tree. The lack of sunlight seemed to affect her the most. She met his eyes, seeing the concern in them, and smiled reassuringly. "But I'm adjusting, thanks to you."

"I want you to be happy here." His eyes told her he didn't quite believe her words, and she didn't know if she believed them, either. Nuzzling her silky cheek against his thick, bare upper arm, she feathered soothing kisses there. "I know being my queen won't always be an easy task."

"I just don't understand what I'm meant to do…"

Aidon slipped his arm around her and kissed the top of her golden head. "You will know when it's time to know."

"Why is it never time for me to know now?" Persephone sounded contrite and childish, even to herself, and she gave him an apologetic smile.

"Being a ruler is about striking a balance between right and wrong, black and white." Aidon gave her a sideways smile. "Pleasure and pain." She returned his smile with a blush. He glanced over to the three judges and then down to where the shades gathered. His eyes grew distant and thoughtful. "Being a ruler is about being a leader, but being a leader isn't about tyranny…it's often about finding a solution that creates the most harmony."

"Is that what you do?"

"I try." He shrugged. "I don't always succeed. It's a balancing act." He chuckled, shaking his head. "It reminds me of Diopeithes."

"Who?"

"Oh, just a juggler at one of Zeus' infamous Mt. Olympus parties." He frowned. "I don't go to them anymore. Anyway, Diopeithes came out with these sticks and plates and did his act for all the gods and goddesses. At first it wasn't that impressive. A pole with a plate spinning on top—big deal. But pretty soon, he had ten, twenty, the whole front of the room filled with these spinning plates."

Persephone stared at him. "Sounds difficult."

"He made it look effortless." He smiled down at her. "As long as he gave each plate the attention it demanded and deserved, he could keep them all going. But then, he got distracted."

"What happened?"

Aidon snorted. "Aphrodite happened. She could distract any god, let alone a man."

"Could she distract you?" Persephone raised her eyebrows.

"Not anymore." He grinned. "But I do like your jealousy."

She rolled her eyes and shook her head. "So what happened?"

"Just what happens when a ruler gets distracted." Aidon shrugged. "All hell broke loose."

"What do you mean?"

"The moment he let his attention slip, one plate crashed into another, and then another, and they all fell like dominos around him."

Persephone blinked, imagining the catastrophic scene. In a little voice, she asked, "Was he punished?"

Aidon shook his head. "Aphrodite found it flattering, so she wouldn't let Zeus punish him too harshly. He just had to clean up his mess."

"I guess that's a fair punishment," she murmured.

Aidon waved the response away. "My point is you have to learn how to juggle, how to keep all the plates in the air at once, and make it look easy."

"No pressure or anything." She made a face at him, turning to look down at the shades below. *What could possibly fill the plates I will have to juggle?*

Aidon lifted her chin and made her look into his eyes. "You already make it look effortless."

"Don't flatter me." For some reason, Persephone thought of her first act as Queen of the Underworld—the pardoning of the man by the front gates. Had she done the right thing? Should she tell Aidon? She opened her mouth to say something when Tisi burst into the Chamber, calling for the King of the Underworld.

"Aidoneus the Unseen, God of the Underworld!" Tisi's voice resounded loud and clear over the murmuring and moaning of the shades.

"Uh-oh." Aidon cringed as Tisi stormed over to his throne, followed by the Moirai—the three Fates. They wrung their hands as they came into the chamber, lagging behind the Fury. The black snakes on the Tisi's head writhed and hissed all at once, as if in some terrible agony. Persephone had never seen Tisi's eyes so red and blazing before.

"Have you heard the call of Althaia, grieved mother of Meleager?" Even Tisi's wings seemed to be quivering with rage.

"I…uh…" Aidon sighed. "I might have heard something…"

"You well know she has been pounding the ground with rocks and calling your name for hours!" Tisi snarled, her fanged teeth flashing white under blood red lips. "Will you not answer her plea?" Tisi stepped forward, her voice dropping to a low hiss almost lost in the sibilance of the snakes curling around her face. "Because if you will not, I promise you, Aidon…I will!"

"Tisi…" Aidon frowned. "You know how little I answer the 'prayers' of mortals. Why should I consider this plea from Althaia? How is it any different from any other human curse? So her son killed both of her brothers, and now, in her grief, she wants him dead… do you really believe she will want the same thing tomorrow, when her head has cleared and her heart has ceased its bleeding?"

The Fury's wings spread wide and she began to take flight. Aidon quickly grasped her hand and held her, shaking his head. "No, Tisi. I know how upset you get about the killing of relatives, but what would this be, but more familial bloodlust? Meleager is Althaia's own son!"

"Aidon, I swear…" Tisi jerked her hand away, her wings still flapping gently, as if she might take off at any moment. "If you do not answer this woman's plea, I will enlist my sisters and we will tear Meleager limb from limb!"

Persephone stared between the two of them, back and forth, her eyes wide. She remembered the two shades Aidon had sent to Elysium—Meleager's uncles. The young hero had killed them, and the whole Underworld had gone to great lengths to keep Tisi from discovering that fact. Now, clearly, she had found out. But how? Persephone leaned in and whispered to Aidon, "I don't understand?"

He glanced over at her with a sigh. "Humans often call to the God of the Dead to curse their enemies. I rarely answer such a call."

"He's afraid to get his hands dirty!" Tisi spat.

Aidon's eyes blazed a bright orange and he stood, towering above the Fury. "I will not cause unnecessary human suffering based on some mortal's emotional whim."

"Justice!" Tisi's voice became a high-pitched screech, so loud Persephone covered her ears in shock and surprise. "I demand justice!"

Aidon shook his head, frowning at the Fury. "No! You want vengeance!"

"Justice! Justice! Justice!" Tisi screamed, the flapping of her wings creating a stir among the shades. The judges had turned their attention to the matter, their eyes on Aidon and the Fury. The shades, too, had turned toward the altercation, shuffling together and watching them.

"The young hero Meleager should already be dead." The thick, cracking voice of Atropos rose as the Moirai came forward. The three Fates never separated, and Clotho and Lachesis followed close behind their sister. "I predicted, when he was but seven days old, he would not live long enough for the stick to burn down in the fire in the hearth."

"Fate is never wrong," Persephone murmured, giving Aidon a puzzled look. "Poor Althaia. Her own son killed both of her brothers. The whole thing is just a tragedy."

"Exactly!" Tisi agreed. "Which is why she's calling for justice!"

Aidon frowned. "I agree it's a tragedy...but why heap more pain and suffering onto the poor woman?"

"Perhaps if she had not tempted Fate to begin with, this would never have happened," Atropos reminded them. Everyone turned to look at the old Moirai, her sisters moving in silently behind her. "Remember, the boy Meleager should have died in infancy. His own mother prevented that, out of her selfishness and trickery. Now look what he has done, what havoc he has wreaked!"

Persephone sighed. "What mother wouldn't try to save her child? Certainly you can't fault the woman for that!"

Aidon nodded slowly and then he turned to the Fury, rubbing his chin thoughtfully. "Tisi...I will answer Althaia's plea."

Surprised, Persephone clutched his arm. "You're not going to let Tisi kill him?"

"No." Aidon glared at the Fury. "Tisi, you will remind Althaia where she hid the stick she took from the fire when Meleager was a babe. And then leave it up to her." Her red eyes blazing, Tisi opened her mouth to protest, but Aidon cut her off. "I mean it, Tisi! No scourges, no teeth, no tearing anyone limb from limb, you got it? If the mother wants her son's death as vengeance, then let her make the choice."

Tisi's whole body seemed to vibrate, her blood-red mouth narrowing into a thin line. She clearly didn't like Aidon's decision, but she didn't say so. "Fine. Consider it done." Her black wings spread wide as she turned and sped out. The Moirai smiled as they departed behind her.

"Tisi wasn't happy." Persephone winced.

"Furies are rarely happy unless they're causing someone pain." Aidon sighed. "It's what they're made to do."

"Well…" She took his hand and squeezed it, giving him a sidelong glance. "Pain isn't such a bad thing sometimes."

He chuckled. "There's a slight difference."

"I know." Lifting her eyes to his, she felt the heat on her cheeks as she remembered. His gaze fell lower to her breasts, and lower still. She loved seeing his eyes begin to glow, a slow smolder. "You are a wise and just ruler, Aidon. I am proud to be your wife." His face softened at her words, saying everything his mouth didn't. His jaw worked and he swallowed, reaching out to rub his thumb over her cheek. "And I understand now what you mean about it being a balancing act."

"Do you?" His smile softened as he leaned down to kiss her. He took her breath every time, thickening her pulse the moment their mouths touched. She slipped her bare leg between his, moaning against his mouth as she squeezed around the thick expanse of his thigh. His growing hardness pressed against her hip and she rubbed along the length of it through his loincloth, making him groan.

He broke the kiss, his eyes on fire. Grabbing a handful of her hair, he tilted her head back and raked his teeth down the sensitive flesh of her throat. She whimpered, biting her lip, and his voice rumbled through her as he growled, "Quit distracting me or everything is going to crash down around our heads."

"Hades!" The voice boomed through the chamber, making them both jump.

Aidon sighed. "See? What did I tell you?" He gave her a wink as he turned toward the source of the thundering voice calling his name.

It was Thanatos, his teeth bared, his eyes almost as red as Tisi's had been. "What in the name of Zeus were you thinking? Sisyphus is now roaming free, bragging to everyone he won't go back to the Underworld until he's a ripe old man!"

"What are you talking about?" Aidon shook his head.

"You know exactly what I'm talking about!" Thanatos hissed. "What did I do to deserve this? Now the little cretin who chained me up in hell for three days is roaming free, back to his old life and his old tricks!"

"Wait a minute." Aidon held up his hand. "You're telling me Sisyphus has left the Underworld?"

Thanatos rolled his eyes. "Don't pretend you don't know what I'm talking about. Only the ruler of the Underworld could have released him from his bond here!"

Persephone had a sinking feeling in her belly as she looked between the two gods, remembering the conversation she'd had with the shade on the banks of the river Styx. It couldn't be…

"I never saw him, Thanatos." Aidon held both hands out now, and shrugged. "I swear to Zeus!"

"Oh, please!" Thanatos bared his massive rows of teeth. "He couldn't have gotten topside without your permission!"

Aidon's eyes began to glow in anger. "Don't doubt me, Thanatos. I am telling you the truth. I never saw the shade!"

"Um…" Persephone poked Aidon in the side. "What…what does this Sisyphus look like?"

He glanced down at her, frowning. "Not now, Persephone."

"Just be god enough to admit it!" Thanatos insisted, folding his arms over his chest. "I want to know what grudge you've got against me! First you leave me chained in Hell for three days, and now you've let the little goathead go free!"

Persephone cleared her throat, her stomach churning as the two gods fought. She tried again, asking in a small voice, "Aidon…this Sisyphus…does he have a moon-like scar on his cheek?"

Both gods stopped and looked at her. Aidon's puzzled eyes moved over her face. "Did you see him, Persephone?"

She nodded, swallowing hard, with both sets of gods' eyes burning into her. "I…uh…" The realization dawned on

Aidon's face, and she saw Thanatos had already made the connection. Still, the words wouldn't come out, as much as she tried to speak them.

"She let him go!" Thanatos smacked his forehead with a groan. "The Queen of the Underworld has gone and granted the little sheep-rustler a pardon!"

Aidon shook his head in disbelief. "Is this true, Persephone?"

"I didn't know." She bit her lip. "He told me his wife left him naked and unburied in the middle of the town square! He only asked to go back and receive a proper burial. It seemed like such a simple request to grant..."

"Brilliant!" Thanatos bared his teeth at her. "And you fell for it?"

"Hey, don't be too hard on her." Aidon held his hand up to the toothy deity. "I seem to remember a certain God of Death who was fooled by the same man."

"You are the fool, Hades!" Thanatos bristled, his eyes bright. "You were blinded by this hussy's beauty! Now you've gone and married her and made this child a Queen!"

"I'm not a child!" Persephone insisted, crossing her arms over her bare chest.

"Thanatos!" Aidon warned, taking a step forward, his eyes blazing. Everyone in the Chamber had stopped to listen to them. Persephone took a step away, the backs of her knees bumping up against the throne made for her. She sat, her trembling legs no longer supporting her.

"She doesn't deserve to sit on the throne!" Thanatos waved his hand at Persephone and she cringed backward into the chair. "You'd better learn to control your new wife, before her tender little heart has the Underworld emptied of shades and the earth roaming with ghosts!"

Persephone sat up straight, her eyes blazing. "Now wait a minute!" Both gods looked at her as she stood, her spine straightening. "Thanatos, I apologize. I made a mistake letting Sisyphus go."

"I'll say," he muttered, crossing his arms. Persephone raised her hand to him and he quieted.

"We are immortal, not perfect." She glanced over at Aidon and saw him looking at her with renewed respect, his eyes bright. "I will do what I can to have Sisyphus returned to the Underworld, and when he does, he will be punished accordingly."

Thanatos gave a curt nod and bowed to her. "Thank you…my queen."

Aidon touched her arm when Thanatos turned to go, his face breaking into a smile. "You are truly my queen."

She smiled up at him as she sank into her throne, her knees still trembling. *I really hope I'm up to this Queen of the Underworld business.* She took a shaky breath as Aidon proudly took his seat beside her and they looked out and surveyed their kingdom.

Chapter Nine

"I heard about Sisyphus." Tisi flashed Persephone a fanged grin as they walked together into the Chamber of Judgment. "I guess he's still refusing to return to Hell...not that I blame him."

"I know. I really felt awful." Persephone still winced when she thought about it. "I didn't mean to let him go. This being Queen of the Underworld thing is pretty complicated."

Tisi laughed, grabbing the goddess' hand and swinging it. "You really got Thannie's goat! I heard he was ready to spit olive pits when he found out!"

Persephone sighed, glancing toward the throne and seeing Aidon deep in discussion with Minos, one of the judges. She and Tisi had spent the afternoon gathering jewels. The rocks near the river Acheron glittered full of them—emeralds, quartz, rubies, even diamonds—and Tisi's claws made perfect tools for extraction. Persephone carried a full, and heavy, black velvet bag she swung against her bare thigh.

"Well, I heard a certain Fury got all ruffled up over some mortal hero's demise."

They both turned at the sound of Thanatos' voice. He lounged under the cypress, his feet up on the trunk, as if sunbathing in the ghostly light of the tree. He quickly rolled to standing, coming toward the pair.

"It was something worth getting ruffled up over." Tisi pulled her teeth back over her fangs at hissed at him. "As far as I'm concerned, you deserved your three days chained in Hell. You're the one who let that old man get the best of you."

"Let him?" Thanatos' teeth flashed just as sharp as Tisi's and infinitely more numerous.

Persephone held up her hand, like she had seen Aidon do, and smiled. "Is there an olive branch in the house?"

Both of them backed off, looking at her a little guiltily. Thanatos gave a slight bow in her direction. "I apologize, Persephone."

"That's Queen Persephone," Tisi reminded him.

Thanatos made a face. "Right. Queen Persephone."

"I should apologize to you again." Persephone nudged Tisi quiet when the Fury opened her mouth. "I never should have made such a snap decision when I didn't know all the factors. I have asked Hecate to search for Sisyphus. I'm sure she will find him soon."

The God of Death frowned, his eyes narrowing as if assessing the sincerity of her statement. "He's gallivanting around up there still, bragging to everyone who will listen about how he chained up the 'Great God of Death.' He's even taken over his own body again!"

"Can't you just…" Persephone made a slicing motion across her slender, bejeweled throat with her finger. "You know…I mean, you are the 'Great God of Death'…"

He ran a hand through his thick, wavy blond hair and sighed. "Believe me, I would if I could."

"Sisyphus isn't alive. Death only applies to the living." Tisi explained with a grin she tried to hide behind her clawed hand. "And since he's not really dead, and he's walking around in his old body…"

"He's undead," Thanatos finished morosely. "I can't touch him."

"Don't worry." Aidon clapped the God of Death on the back with a wink and slipped his arm around his wife's waist. Persephone smiled up at him, nudging her naked hip against his thigh. "We'll drag him back here by his oily little head if we have to."

"And then?"

"We'll make an example of him," Aidon assured him. "Persephone probably did us a favor. They'll tell the story of Sisyphus for generations, and shades everywhere will shudder at the mention of his name. No one will ever try to escape the Underworld again."

Thanatos considered this. "What will we do to him?"

Tisi's eyes flashed red and she licked her lips. "I can tear him limb from—"

"He won't have any limbs, Tisi," Aidon reminded her, shooting her a quelling look.

"Oh, right." She grinned sheepishly. "Sorry, I'm so used to mortal punishment…"

"How about chaining him up forever?" Thanatos asked, his eyes flashing. "Now that's poetic justice."

"Please use your imagination, Thannie." Tisi rolled her eyes. "We can do better than that."

"Well, now my mind is going to chains, as well…" Aidon's eyes moved over Persephone's nude form and he grinned.

"Men!" Persephone threw up her hands. "I have the perfect punishment. No swimming in the Pool of Lethe for Sisyphus. He can keep forever the memory of the earthly world as he pushes a rock uphill."

"Feh!" Aidon waved her idea away with a snort. "What kind of punishment is that?"

Persephone glared at him. "I'm not finished. He can push a rock uphill for all eternity. When he gets to the top of the hill, the rock will roll down, so he'll have to start all over again…and again…and again…"

Aidon stared at her, his mouth agape. "That's…truly cruel."

"Diabolical." Tisi gave Persephone an appreciative wink.

"Brilliant!" The God of Death grinned over at Aidon, all of his razor sharp teeth showing. "I take back what I said about questioning your choice…she is the quintessential Queen of the Underworld."

Aidon's hand rubbed Persephone's hip and their eyes met. The warmth that passed between them was nearly tangible and she felt her skin tingling when he said, "I knew it the moment I saw her."

She remembered that day in the clearing with a small, secret smile. That restless, yearning girl who had rolled in the grass with goddesses for hours still unsatisfied was no more. How far she had come, in such a short time. She wondered if anyone from home would even recognize her anymore, branded with tattoos, wearing the dark coal liner Hecate had taught her to use to accent her eyes.

"In light of your clever plan, I have a task for you, my queen." Aidon took her hand and lifted her palm to his lips, kissing her there. Whenever his lips touched her skin, all thought seemed to leave her head. "Will you come with me?"

She knew she would follow him anywhere as they made their way toward the Judges' bench. Aidon looked back over his shoulder at Tisiphone and Thanatos, "Come on, you two."

Tisi shrugged but she fell in line behind them and stood aside with the God of Death as the two rulers took their thrones on the platform above.

Aidon nodded toward Minos and he waved two shades toward them. The women cried and clung together, their graying outlines colorless and hazily transparent. Persephone looked, puzzled, between Aidon and the two huddled figures who stopped in front of her throne.

"Althaia, mother of the fallen Meleager, and Cleopatra, his wife." Aidon nodded to the older and younger woman respectively, making introductions and directing them in a loud voice. "Kneel before the Queen of the Underworld!"

Trembling, both of them fell to their knees, still holding and rocking one another. The tears ran down their gray cheeks like quicksilver, falling in beaded splashes like mercury on the black onyx floor. Persephone thought she understood what Aidon was going to ask, and she gulped, glancing toward the three tunnels that led to the destination points of the shades. Hecate stood at the entrance wearing a robe and hood, her torch blazing as she directed the dead to their final fates: the fires of Tartarus, the paradise of Elysium, or the gray, dull plains of Asphodel.

"Please, spare us the hell of Tartarus!" Althaia's voice quavered in the muted tone of the dead. "That is all I humbly ask, my queen."

Aidon leaned over and murmured, "Do what you feel is best."

Persephone frowned at them both. "How did you come to be here among the unliving? Meleager passed this way two days ago." She hadn't seen the young hero, but Aidon had sighed when he told her about it, relaying his own disappointment in Althaia's decision to burn the stick that would take her own son's life.

Althaia put her arm around the younger woman, whose sobs seemed to fill the room at the question, attempting in vain to comfort her. "I made a grievous error, Queen Persephone. In my grief and anger at my son for killing my brothers, his own uncles..." The woman's lower lip trembled and she hesitated, as if saying the words caused her pain. "One of the Erinyes reminded me of a stick the Fates predicted would kill Meleager if it were left to burn in the fire when he was a babe." Tisi shrugged at the woman, but the Fury looked a little guilty when she met Aidon's eyes.

"In a fit of anger, I dug up the stick and threw it into the fire." Althaia lowered her head, her voice choked and low. "I tried to take it back..." The woman showed Persephone her hands, blistered and blackened by the fire. "But it was too late...my son was already dead."

"That explains your son's death." Persephone nodded. "But yours?"

"I couldn't live with my guilt or my grief." Althaia's voice wavered. "I took my own life."

Persephone's eyes went to the younger woman. "And you?"

"I took my own life, as well." Cleopatra spoke for the first time, her small voice pained and hoarse. "I couldn't live without my Meleager." She turned and buried her face against the older woman's shoulder, sobbing again.

"Do you not want revenge against your mother-in-law?" Persephone inquired. Cleopatra raised her tear-stained cheeks, her eyes wide. "She is the one who took your husband from you."

"No, of course not!" The young woman gave her a startled look. "I understand her pain. She lost two brothers. Yes, I know what it is like to lose someone you love and feel that helpless, hopeless rage…but what good is it to injure someone already so troubled herself?"

Althaia kissed her daughter-in-law's cheek. "You are wise, child. I am such an old fool."

Persephone looked between the two women, considering. "Althaia, you made a hasty, unwise decision in your overly emotional state, and I am sorry for it, as are you. But Cleopatra, you have ended this cycle of vengeance, and for that I am glad, and you will thus be spared the fires of Tartarus."

The two women hugged and sobbed again, this time for joy. Persephone held up her hand, shaking her head. "However…you will not swim in the Pool of Lethe. You will forever remember your loved ones, and what part you played in this mortal drama."

"Thank you, Queen Persephone!" Althaia touched her forehead to the top of Persephone's bare foot. "You are most merciful."

Cleopatra did the same, tenderly kissing the side of Persephone's slim ankle. On a whim, the blonde goddess leaned down and whispered into the shade's ear, "The good news is you're going to Asphodel, and you will remember your husband, Meleager…he is there." The woman's eyes brightened as she stood, smiling for the first time.

"Go!" Persephone waved them off. "To the fields of Asphodel with you!"

Both of them turned and fled toward Hecate, bypassing the Pool of Lethe. Persephone glanced at Aidon, who looked so proud he might have popped a button on his vest—if he wore one.

"Perfect." He touched the tip of her nose with his finger. "Inside and out."

Thanatos approached their thrones and knelt before Persephone, bowing his head low. "My queen." No hint of sarcasm remained in his voice as he lifted his eyes to hers. "I apologize. You are more than worthy."

"Thank you." She smiled and touched his hand. "Now get up, 'Great God of Death,' I know you must have work to do. We have more shades down here lately than we can count!"

He laughed, delighted, giving her a wink as he stood. "As you wish!" He gave Aidon and Tisi a wave and disappeared—literally, just disappeared!

"I didn't know he could do that!" Persephone gasped, her eyes wide.

Aidon chuckled. "Death can sneak up on you at any time."

"Speaking of apologies…" Persephone looked over to where the two women she had sent to Asphodel passed Hecate's hooded form. "There's someone I have to speak to. Would you excuse me?"

Aidon frowned. "Be careful."

She didn't reply as she made her way across the Chamber of Judgment. Hecate had put her torch up on the wall and headed now toward the exit. *Where is she going?* Persephone hurried to catch up.

"Hecate!" Persephone called after the goddess, running in bare feet over the rocky surface to catch up to her. They hadn't spoken since that day by the Styx, and by the time Persephone caught up to her, they were on the banks of the river once again. She put her hand on Hecate's arm, out of breath, as Charon pulled his skiff to shore. "Where are you rushing off to?"

She never knew which of Hecate's faces she would see—young maiden, matronly mother, or old crone. The triple goddess pushed her hood back, and Persephone saw the wrinkled face of an old witch, with wise, bright eyes. The old woman inclined her head and smiled warmly. "I promised Zeus I'd run a quick errand for him. I'll be back before you know it, my queen."

"Will I ever grow used to that title?" Persephone laughed. "Hecate, dearest, I wanted to apologize for the other day."

The old woman waved her mottled hand. "Pish! Is that what you ran down here for? Think nothing of it."

Persephone shook her head. "No, really. I shouldn't have said such things to you. And Demeter is my mother, she deserves to know what happened. I will tell her where I am...soon. I promise."

Hecate eyed the young goddess. "It is well, then. She grieves piteously for you now."

Persephone felt tears welling up in her eyes. "Thank you for telling me."

Hecate kissed a tear on Persephone's cheek. "You are welcome, my queen. And you well deserve the title, so you'd best get used to it."

More tears fell from Persephone's eyes and she hugged the old woman tightly. "You are pure sweetness, Hecate."

The old woman snorted. "The shades I guide to Tartarus do not think so." But her face blushed a rosy pink and she faded slightly out of Persephone's vision as they parted, like she always did when anxious or embarrassed.

"It's a useful skill, becoming invisible," Persephone observed with a smile as the old woman became solid again. "Thanatos just blinked out of here, too!"

"It can be." Hecate cackled as she stepped onto the skiff while a boatload of shades shuffled off, calling, "Your husband certainly loves the helmet Hephaestus made for him!"

Waving, Persephone remembered that day in the meadow, when Aidon had used his helmet to conceal himself from her. *How often does he use it?* she wondered with a frown.

Her mind didn't have time to linger on the thought. Behind her, a voice that didn't belong to her husband spoke much too close to her ear for comfort. "I told you I would have you." A memory flashed across her mind at the sound and she whirled around, coming face-to-face with the man.

Chapter Ten

"Pirithous?"

Had she really forgotten? How long had it been since that day in the woods? It was the day Aidon had come for her, the day her innocence was lost forever. She had never expected to see this man again, and yet here he was, his eyes raking over her nude form. His gaze made her long for covering like she rarely did down here. *How is this possible?*

"What are you doing here?"

"I came to make you my bride." His grin widened, his eyes blazing with triumph. Behind him stood another man, who watched with a quiet frown on his face. Persephone didn't recognize him. She glanced across the river, thinking to call to Hecate, but the goddess was already gone.

"You're too late. I am already a bride." She fought the urge to cover herself and lifted her chin higher. "I am Queen of the Underworld. Now, please depart. Mortals are not welcome in this place." In spite of the burning ball of fire in her belly, she attempted to dismiss them with a haughty wave of her hand, brushing quickly by. If she could just make it past Cerberus and into the Chamber of Judgment...

A hand grabbed her hair and she screamed as Pirithous pulled her back against his barrel chest. "You always did think you were too good for me, you lofty little bitch!" He kissed her hard, forcing his tongue deep into her throat. She gagged, the memory in the woods hitting her full force. Trying to scream, she twisted in his arms, but he wouldn't let her go.

"Pardon me."

Aidon! Oh thank the gods! But where had he come from? Relief flooded her belly as she turned to him. He leaned casually against the rocky wall, which was glowing a deep red behind him. When she saw a golden helmet tucked under his arm, she understood—but how long had he been there? She tried to go to him, but Pirithous held her fast.

"Might I ask what you two are doing down here in the Underworld?" Aidon looked at the man who squeezed Persephone's arm. "Pirithous?" His eyes went to the quiet figure standing slightly apart. "Theseus?"

Theseus! Even in her sheltered existence, Persephone had heard of this mortal's deeds in the labyrinth with the Minotaur. She glanced at him, frowning.

Pirithous put his arm around Persephone's shoulder and smiled widely at Aidon. "I have come to deliver the Goddess of Spring and my promised bride back to her waiting mother."

"Have you now?" Aidon raised his eyebrows in mild surprise. "And how do I know you're speaking the truth? You obviously had to trick your way into my realm somehow…why should I trust you?"

Pirithous reached into his robe and pulled out a wooden box, opening it up. "I have this." Inside rested a golden heart attached to a delicate chain. It glowed a soft blue around the edges. Persephone gasped, her hand going to her mouth, her eyes wide. The older man smiled. "This is Persephone's most prized possession, given to her by Demeter as protection. The young goddess gave it to me and promised to be my bride before you abducted her against her will."

"Aidon!" Persephone protested. "You cannot—"

He held up a hand to her, shaking his head. His eyes glowed a deep, dark orange she had come to know as smoldering anger. He grabbed the necklace out of the box.

"No!" she screamed, lunging for it. The blue glow had increased since Pirithous opened the box and she thought it would knock Aidon backwards, the way it had the old man in the woods. She stared, stunned, as the blue glow faded when Aidon dangled the chain from his fingers. *How is that possible?*

He held it up in her face, demanding, "Persephone, do you recognize this charm?"

"Yes, but—"

Pirithous stepped forward, putting his arm around the goddess. "She is afraid of your wrath now and will deny it, I'm sure. But before you came, she was sobbing to me, begging to be rescued from this demon's lair."

"I was not!" Persephone gasped, her eyes wide.

"You see." Pirithous shrugged. "Demeter has sent me to retrieve her only daughter. I have her full blessing."

Aidon frowned at the man, looking at the necklace in his hand. "Is that so?"

Pirithous' eyes narrowed. "You should know all of the gods and goddesses alike are up in arms about your abduction and rape of this poor young goddess."

Aidon stood fully, his eyes blazing, and gave a curt nod. "Well, then, gentlemen, follow me." His eyes skipped over to Persephone for just a moment. "Let's order a feast to celebrate your impending marriage to Pirithous before you go."

The two middle-aged heroes looked almost as shocked as Persephone herself. They stared open-mouthed at one another for a moment until Aidon turned back and called them again.

"Come on!" He waved them over and got them moving.

Persephone, stunned, followed meekly, her eyes burning with unshed tears. Did Aidon really mean to give her to this man? She couldn't let that happen! She knew she had to find a way to speak to him alone somehow, and quickly. He couldn't possibly believe…

"So how long have you and Persephone known each other?" Aidon led them through the rocky crevasse and down the long flight of stairs where Cerberus waited.

"Not long," Pirithous admitted, glancing over Theseus and shrugging when the man shot him a puzzled look. "Theseus and I found ourselves without companionship in our mid-years, and we both decided we were heroes worthy of now claiming a daughter of Zeus."

"Is that so?" Aidon stopped Cerberus' growl with a wave of his hand, and the dog sat, panting as he scratched him behind each floppy black ear. "Are you both to marry her, then?"

"No." Theseus spoke for the first time. "I chose young Helen—daughter of Zeus and the fair Leda. We...er...acquired her...about a month ago..."

"She's only ten years old!" Persephone knew the girl from Demeter's stories of Zeus' many philandering exploits. Helen was the product of Zeus' attempt to seduce Leda by turning himself into a swan. Persephone's panicked eyes skipped over to Aidon. "She is nowhere near marriageable age!"

Theseus smiled a little sheepishly. "Yes. I know, but I swear she will be the most beautiful woman in the world some day. I saw her in Artemis' temple and knew I had to have her. I left her with my mother, Aethra, and she will keep her for me until the girl can marry."

"Good thinking." Aidon nodded, patting Cerberus on the head.

"What?" Persephone stared at Aidon. "You're praising the kidnapping of a young girl?"

"Come along." Aidon stepped into the Chamber of Judgment and they all followed. "Frankly, it doesn't surprise me to hear there was a prior arrangement Persephone didn't inform me about. I'll be glad to get rid of her. She's quite a handful. Good luck to you, Pirithous."

The older man grinned. "She's proud, I'll grant you that. But breaking her will be such a pleasure." He slipped his arm around Persephone's shoulder and squeezed. She glared at him and slid away from his grasp, her heart pounding in her chest at Aidon's words.

Aidon didn't reply to the man, stopping to speak to one of the Keres. Aidon squatted down to speak to them in a low voice, and they turned their dark eyes up to him in unison. Petulantia always looked as if she wanted to swallow Aidon whole. Persephone had never liked the way the Ker rubbed up against him. Her thick, snake-like arms could coil around his thighs three times, and often did before he even noticed.

Persephone knew they used the tactic to hold their mortal prey.

"Follow me to the Great Hall." Aidon stood, giving a nod to the three Keres as they scurried away. "A feast is being prepared in honor of your upcoming nuptials, Pirithous."

Persephone couldn't believe her ears. Had she really heard Aidon tell this old man he would be glad to be rid of her? *He can't mean it!* She tried to catch his eye, to find any sign, a wink, something to prove this some sort of ruse. Aidon tucked his helmet under his arm and opened a tall, heavy door with the other. Persephone had been into the Great Hall only once. Most of their meals were taken in chambers. They had never had the occasion or opportunity to use it, aside from the day of their wedding.

She hurried to catch up to him, determined to tell him the truth, to lay any doubts he might have at rest. Putting her hand on his arm, she murmured, "Aidon, please…we have to talk."

"You clearly want to be rescued from my horrible clutches." He glanced down at her, shaking her hand off his arm and tossing his helmet onto the table. "I'm sure you will be quite happy with King Pirithous, Persephone." His voice deepened as he pressed her into a chair, his hand tightening almost to the point of pain on her shoulder. "I'm afraid our guest list is rather small. It was such short notice and this is, after all, the Underworld. We are rather short on live humans." Aidon nodded toward a bench across from Persephone. "But I insist the two mortals take a seat as my guests of honor." Theseus shrugged at Pirithous and they both sat down, side by side, on the bright, golden colored bench.

Persephone's head whirled, and she turned her face up to Aidon's, pleading with her eyes. "Aidon, you have to believe me…" He ignored her whispered words, his jaw working as he took a seat at the head of the table. Miseria brought them a carafe of wine and four goblets.

"So what took you so long?" Aidon poured the wine, glancing over at the two men. "Persephone has been here…how long has it been, now?"

"Three months." Pirithous took the offered glass and gulped greedily. Persephone met Aidon's eyes briefly. Could it really have been so long?

Theseus sighed. "We got tied up for a while in the Calydonian Boar Hunt. Piri insisted." He accepted the goblet Aidon offered him with a nod.

"Meleager was an Argonaut, the same as I was!" Pirithous reminded him with a frown. "I owed him that, anyway."

"And how did he repay you?" Theseus scoffed. "By giving the prize boar hide to a woman!"

Aidon slid a full glass across to Persephone. Their fingers brushed and she looked hopefully at him, but then Petulantia entered the Great Hall, slipping up beside Aidon to whisper something into his ear, diverting his attention.

"Thank you, Pet." He patted her on the head and stood, grabbing his helmet off the table. "Gentlemen, excuse me for a moment. I'll be right back." Aidon shook Petulantia off his leg, where her arms already stretched like taffy, around and around. She let go reluctantly, pouting after him as he opened the heavy door to the Great Hall, leaving it slightly ajar as he left.

Persephone watched, wide-eyed, her heart beating a thick pulse in her throat. This couldn't be happening. She turned to Pirithous, her eyes narrowing as he poured himself another goblet of wine and raised it to her.

"To our wedding." He winked and downed the liquid in two huge gulps, wiping his mouth with the back of his hand and grinning across the table at her. Then he belched and added, "And especially to our wedding night."

"I've already had my wedding night, and believe me when I tell you…" Persephone's lip curled in a sneer. "You could not compare."

Pirithous shrugged. "Now that you're damaged goods, you are even more valuable to me. I'm sure Demeter will be so grateful to have her wayward daughter back, she will increase your wedding inheritance tenfold when I tell her you were raped by the God of the Underworld before I could rescue you." He leaned over and winked and nudged at Theseus. "And I won't have to wrestle with her and get blood on my sheets."

"I will not go with you." Persephone hid her clenched hands in her lap, her eyes moving from one man to the other.

"You don't have a choice." Pirithous crossed his arms and smiled at her. "Besides, he seems eager enough to let you go."

The words made her heart lurch and she glanced again toward the door where Aidon had disappeared. It stood open now, the hallway empty. *Does he really mean to let them take me? I can't believe it.* "You know I don't want to go with you! I never begged you to be rescued!"

Theseus leaned his elbow on the table and rested his chin on his hand, giving her a puzzled look. "Why would you want to stay in this dismal place, goddess? You were meant for much brighter surroundings than these!"

"Looks can be deceiving." As she said the words, she glanced again toward the door, thinking of Aidon. *Looks can be deceiving. Surely that's the case here,* she reasoned. *Aidon's planning something. He has to be.* If she trusted him, if she loved him…

Pirithous let out a yelp of laughter. "Please! You can't tell me you have feelings for… that…that…monster?" He waved his hand toward the door where Aidon had disappeared.

"I love him." She spoke the words in soft realization. Tears stung her eyes and she willed them not to fall. She knew how it must look. To the rest of the world, Aidon was the man who had kidnapped her, punished her, stolen her innocence and forced her to bend to his will. To her, he was the man who had taken her, opened her, ravished her, and exposed her to a whole new world of pleasurable pain beyond any sweetness or light she had ever experienced.

"You are naïve, aren't you?" Pirithous whistled and hooked his thumbs together, flapping his fingers like wings. "Look, Theseus, the little bird's fallen in love with her captor."

"You should be thanking us, goddess." Theseus nudged his friend quiet. "Your mother will be very grateful to have you home. Don't you miss her?"

"I am home." Persephone stood, leveling her eyes at them, her voice clear and strong. "And I will thank you to leave it. Now." She pointed toward the open door and waited.

Pirithous leaned back on the bench, draping his arm over his friend's shoulders. "I'm afraid we're not going anywhere, princess. Not without you."

Theseus, frowning, leaned over to speak to his friend. "Piri, maybe this isn't such a good idea."

"Don't you back down on me, now, you coward!" Pirithous growled. "You agreed you would help me if I got the girl for you!"

"I know..." Theseus swallowed. "But maybe that wasn't such a good idea, either. We were pretty drunk the night we made these plans..."

Pirithous glowered at him. "Well, maybe you're getting cold feet, but I'm not going to give up my prize!"

"I'm not your prize!" Persephone cried. "Aidon will never let you take me!"

"You are a foolish girl," Pirithous laughed. "Do you think the God of the Underworld is going to listen to you? Do you really think he's going to believe a woman over a king—a hero?" He snorted and finished his wine. "He doesn't deserve my prize! I'm better than he is!"

Theseus' eyes widened. "Piri, maybe we shouldn't—"

"Oh shut up, you coward!" Pirithous shoved his friend. "I deserve her and you know it! I should be a god—I'm better than a god! I'm going to steal this bright beauty right out from under the God of the Underworld's nose, and the whole of Greece will talk about how Pirithous cheated Hell itself!"

"I'm afraid not." Aidon's voice came out of thin air and they all turned their heads at once in the direction it seemed to be coming from. His image shimmered before them for a moment and Persephone saw him taking off the golden helmet he had been wearing. "Your dreams of grandeur have just been cancelled."

Both Theseus and Pirithous reacted as warriors, reaching for their swords and moving to stand, but neither of them budged from the bench they sat on. The startled look that passed between them was almost comical. If Persephone hadn't been so surprised by their ineffectual attempt at rising, she would have laughed out loud. It wasn't until she moved closer to Aidon that she saw the flexible arms of the Keres wrapped securely around and around their ankles and calves, tethering them to the legs of the bench.

"Swords won't do you any good." Aidon stepped forward and quickly disarmed both heroes, tossing the heavy blades on the long obsidian table. "The Keres are immortal and their limbs are regenerative. You can't escape their grip."

"I can't feel my legs!" Theseus gasped, struggling in Miseria's grasp. The Ker licked her lips and salivated at the sight of his twisting body. He attempted to pry her coiled arms off to no avail.

"What do you mean to do to us?" Pirithous' face turned waxy under his salt and pepper beard, his eyes on Aidon.

"You came here thinking to steal what belongs here." Aidon slipped his arm around Persephone's waist, pulling her close. "No one leaves with the riches of the Underworld." Aidon's eyes met hers and his face softened. "This is the most precious jewel in my kingdom."

"Aidon…" She leaned her head against him, feeling tears welling up again. Her words felt caught in her throat.

He kissed the top of her head and held her to him with one arm.

"Tisi!" He called for the Fury and she appeared, almost as if she had been waiting just outside the door. When Tisi winked in her direction, Persephone realized waiting outside the door was exactly what the Fury had been doing. "You've been itching to tear someone limb from limb?"

Tisi grinned, her sharp fangs flashing. "Oh please, can't I have them both?"

Aidon shook his head. "Just this one." He waved his hand at Pirithous and then met Tisi's glowing, red eyes. "I don't care what you do to him…just do it slowly."

The Fury smiled. "Your wish is my command."

"But Master…" Petulantia turned her lustful eyes up to Aidon. "Can't we have him?"

"Not this time." His smile twisted cruelly. "You are too quick to give a soul to me in order to feast on the body."

Pirithous' eyes widened as he looked between the Fury and the Keres. He looked at Persephone, pleading. "Please…Queen Persephone…please don't let them do this. I beg you."

"Mortals who aspire to be gods deserve a Fury's justice," Persephone said, shaking her head. "I'm sorry, I can't help you."

"However…" Aidon smiled, squatting down by the Keres. "When Tisi is through with the torture, you may have what is left of him." They all seemed to hum in appreciation at once, and to Persephone, they sounded like kittens mewing in pleasure.

"Meg! Alec!" Tisi's voice brought her sisters sailing into the room. They both tucked their wings in behind them as they landed. Tisi winked at Persephone. "I can't have all the fun!"

"Let him go, Pet." Aidon nudged Petulantia, and the Ker sighed and slowly withdrew her long limbs. Pirithous sprang up quickly, reaching for his sword, but Tisi's clawed hand was too quick. Her sharp talons dug into the man's shoulder and he screamed, the sound piercing in the huge room.

"Not yet, little mouse." Tisi nodded to her sisters and they dug in as well, grabbing onto the man's flesh with their claws. Persephone looked away at the sight of his blood, but the Keres licked their lips. "We're going to go play!" With that, the Furies all spread their wings. They carried the wailing and sobbing Pirithous between them as they flew together out of the Great Hall.

Theseus hung his head, looking defeated. "What is to be my fate, then?"

Aidon, still squatting down by the Keres, met the hero's eyes. "I should probably have you killed as well. Taking and keeping a ten-year-old girl to be your future bride?" He shook his dark head, his eyes glowing with anger. "Pet, would you do me a favor?" Petulantia's long limbs began to wrap themselves around him. "Would you send Hecate to me? Then you can go on and find the Furies and watch the fun."

"Yes, Master!" The Ker scurried quickly off, leaving her sisters still clinging to Theseus' legs without a second glance.

"I'm afraid you won't be going anywhere, either, friend." Aidon stood, speaking to Theseus, and then called over his shoulder. "Hypnos!"

Persephone gasped as the God of Sleep came out of the shadows. She had only ever seen him twice—that first night, and again at her wedding. His gaunt, pale cheeks and red, smiling mouth contrasted with the huge, deep pools of his eyes as he glided forward, almost as if walking on air.

"Put him to sleep." Aidon glared at Theseus.

"For how long?" Hypnos' spoke in a hushed tone, barely a whisper, yet somehow melodic.

Aidon considered this. "Can you give him the sleep of forgetfulness?"

"Yes…but he must not be removed from his place of slumber, or he will wake and remember." Hypnos approached the frightened hero, his voice soft and hypnotic. "Do not be afraid…it's just sleep…sink into it…there…that's very good…"

Persephone watched, amazed, as Theseus' lids grew heavy and the God of Sleep slipped a few crystals from a vial under the man's tongue. It wasn't long before Theseus was motionless, head thrown back, arms resting on the back of the bench, his breathing deep and even.

"I am here!" Hecate appeared out of nowhere and Persephone gasped out loud.

"I wish people would stop doing that!" She jumped back, her hand going to the ruby at her throat.

"Sorry." Hecate apologized, flashing her a matronly smile. A rounded, mother figure today, her cheeks glowed full and rosy, her hips broad and full.

"Hecate, I need a favor." Aidon nodded at Theseus. "See that?"

The triple goddess raised her eyebrows. "The young hero Theseus. What has he done to gain your disfavor?"

"Among other things, not the least of which was attempting to kidnap my wife…" Aidon's eyes met Persephone's. "He has also taken Leda's young Helen and hid her away at his mother's."

"For what purpose?"

Persephone grimaced. "He was going to keep her until she was of marriageable age."

"Poor girl!" Hecate gasped, her motherly instincts in full swing. "Where is she? I'll go get her right now!"

Aidon sighed. "Hecate, calm down. Just go tell Helen's brother, Polydeuces, and her half-brother, Castor, where she is. They'll go get her, I promise you."

"Oh, all right." The goddess blinked out of sight entirely.

"Either I need to learn how to do that," Persephone sighed, "or people need to just stop it!"

Aidon grinned. "Maybe I'll let you borrow my invisibility helmet again."

"That was sneaky!" She nudged him with a laugh. "How long were you standing there?"

He pulled her into his arms, nuzzling his face against her hair. "Long enough to hear you say you loved me."

"You heard that?" She smiled up at him, blushing.

"Yes." He cupped her face in his hands, his eyes searching hers. "I love you, too, you know. Did you really believe I would let him take you?" He kissed her, not even giving her time to answer the question. Her body melted into his, her mouth seeking more of him, their tongues touching, making her moan softly. She stretched up on tiptoe, slipping her arm around his neck, begging for more with every inch of her body.

"Master?" The voice startled them both and Persephone looked guiltily toward the Keres, Miseria and Discordia, their arms still wrapped around the sleeping Theseus, holding him fast to the bench.

"Oh right." Aidon sighed, letting Persephone go and walking over toward them. "Girls, I have good news and bad news. The bad news is…I kind of need you to hang onto him…for all eternity." Miseria's eyes welled up with tears. "The good news is…all I need is your arms." The look of realization dawned on Discordia's face and Aidon winced. "They'll grow back in a few days, right?"

Miseria looked up as if expecting nothing else as Aidon brought a sword down, severing her arms. He did the same to Discordia, and both Keres moved away from the bench as the arms still wrapped around Theseus bled for a moment and then stopped.

"I'm sorry." Aidon patted Miseria on the head as she licked at her stump. "But I'm sure Tisi will toss you lots of good scraps!" At that, both Keres scurried after the Furies, forgetting all about their missing limbs.

Aidon turned to Persephone, holding up the locket. "I believe this belongs to you?"

She took it from him, shaking her head and touching the ruby at her throat. "I have another now."

"So you did not beg to be rescued?" Aidon asked. "You do not want to go home to your mother?"

"Come with me." Persephone led him out of the Great Hall and into the Chamber of Judgment. She stood over the Pool of Lethe, dangling her mother's necklace for a moment before letting it drop into the depths. "Actions speak louder than words."

"Yes, they do." Aidon pulled her into his arms, kissing her deeply. "Now let me take you to bed and show you some more action." She laughed and wrapped her arms around his neck as he swept her up, carrying her off to their bed chamber.

Chapter Eleven

"What—?" The question died on her lips as he slipped a smooth, round object inside of her, pressing it deep with his finger. Persephone wiggled on the bed as he slid another in, the balls sliding together inside of her.

"Hold them there." He removed his finger slowly, and she tightened her muscles, feeling the balls inside of her shift and move as they settled. Aidon watched her face as his finger traced between her lips, moving toward the top of her cleft and circling the little nub of flesh there. He rubbed her little omi until she flushed, breathing fast, her eyes half-closed in pleasure.

"Stand up." Stopping abruptly, he backed away from the bed. Persephone bit her lip and squirmed, sitting up on the bed. She felt the rounded objects inside of her slipping downward and she gasped, tightening her muscles. Aidon nodded, smiling. "Don't let them fall."

She took his hand and let him help her from the bed, her eyes wide as she began to follow him. The two balls rubbed together as she walked, giving her a feeling of fullness. Keeping the muscles there tight, she pressed close to him and he kissed her, grabbing her hair and pulling it back in his fist.

"Stand up on the bed." Aidon walked over to the cabinet in the corner, not even turning to check if she would follow his instruction.

She looked back at the huge piece of furniture. Persephone had never seen a bed like theirs before. Black metal posts sunk into the floor and ran straight up into the ceiling to make for the bed's frame. Chains hung from the top and bottom of each post. She worked to get up on the high mattress without letting go of the objects between her legs. Turning backwards, she slid her bottom up on the edge, wiggling back.

"Stand up." Aidon stood at the foot of the bed and waited for her to struggle to standing, the weighted balls inside of her shifting as she used one of the bedposts for balance.

"Face me." He slipped a leather strap around one of her wrists. Lined with soft fleece, it created a very different sensation from the shackles and chains she had been in earlier. She stood taller than him now at the edge of the mattress as he clasped a matching leather bracelet around her other wrist, buckling it closed. Hooking each wrist to one of the chains on the bedposts, Aidon adjusted the length so her arms opened wide.

"Spread your legs." He waited while she opened her thighs, slowly sliding her feet apart. She felt the heavy spheres inside of her beginning to slip downward and she bit her lip, tightening her muscles and stopping their motion. One of them slipped to the opening of her lips, and she felt it bulging outward slightly. Looking down, she saw Aidon's eyes focused between her legs.

"Don't let them fall," he warned as he buckled a matching set of padded leather straps around her ankles and chained her feet apart as well. Persephone's lower belly fluttered as she tensed all of her muscles to hold onto the orbs he had placed inside of her sex. The feeling of fullness grew incredible, focusing all of her attention in her pelvis, although she became acutely aware of how exposed and vulnerable she felt, standing naked and chained to the bedposts.

An oversized chair sat in the corner, upholstered in a soft, dark material. Aidon pulled it over and placed it directly in front of her. Persephone whimpered as he sat in it and leaned back, his eyes moving slowly over her nude form, top to bottom. He seemed to be in no hurry as he studied her, watching her strain to keep the orbs tucked up inside of her.

"Hephaestus is a good friend of mine," Aidon told her, seemingly apropos of nothing. His hand moved over the dark loincloth he wore, and Persephone saw the growing bulge beneath it. He was clearly exciting by her predicament. She watched as he pulled something out of a pocket in the side, a small rectangle. "He made those golden orbs I put inside of you."

Persephone's eyes widened just slightly. She remembered the golden phallus Athena had shown her in the field. Now the reference to Hephaestus made a great deal of sense, and before she had time to wonder if these metal balls held the same magic, they began to hum.

"Ohhhhh, great merciful Zeus!" she moaned as the orbs vibrated faster, controlled by the rectangle in Aidon's hand.

"Great…merciful…who?"

"Aidon!" Persephone cried as the buzzing increased a little further.

He chuckled. "That's better." Resting the controls on the arm of the chair, Aidon slid his hand beneath the dark loincloth, and she saw him touching himself through the material. The memory of him moving inside of her brought a flush to her cheeks, and she was ashamed at how much she found herself wanting it again. An incredible heat grew between her legs, and although the steady hum inside of her sex felt good, it served more to drive her to distraction than anything else.

"It will get even more difficult." Aidon's hand shuttled faster up and down his length, and she couldn't take her eyes off the motion. She found herself wanting to see him and wished he would take the loincloth off completely. "As you get wetter, those golden orbs will get harder to hold."

He was right. Her sex pulsed with a thick heat. It felt swollen, and the humming deep inside made her breath come faster and her cheeks flush. She had to tighten her muscles around the vibrating orbs and it just served to increase the sensation through her pelvis.

"You are getting wetter, aren't you, Sephie?"

"Yes, Aidon." She squirmed, her body pulling against the restraints as she struggled to maintain the hold on the slippery spheres sliding inside her sex. He watched her, a half-smile on his face, his hand moving in a steady rhythm between his own thighs. She couldn't stand it anymore! "Oh please...I want..."

"I know." His smile changed, twisting into something almost cruel, his eyes glowing in the dimness. "I know exactly what you want. And I'll give it to you...when I'm ready...and when you are."

"Please!" she begged, her hips thrusting forward all on their own. "I'm ready!"

"No." He shook his head, the smile never leaving his face. "I'll tell you when you're ready."

Groaning, she hung her head, defeated, the aching hum making her whole body tremble in the chains that held her aloft. *This is torture! Sweet, delicious, horrible torture!* She glanced at him again and licked her lips, watching with fascinated eyes at the movement of his hand. She longed to touch herself, too, to ease that precious ache.

"You like watching," he observed, easing back in the chair and pushing his hips up. The bulge there was very noticeable and she nodded. She couldn't deny it. When he reached over and untied the loin cloth, exposing his hard length, she groaned out loud. She had never wanted anything more in her life. He pressed his erection up toward his belly, rubbing the wet tip of it there, and she watched as he took himself in hand. The motion hypnotized her, up and down, growing faster with his breath, and then slowing again. She remembered how it felt in her mouth, the thick pulse of him throbbing in her throat, and it made her mouth water.

"Please..." she whispered, arching forward in the chains, straining toward him.

"I like hearing you say please." He smiled, his eyes meeting hers. "It's such a pretty word from that pretty little mouth." His gaze lingered over her mouth and then swept downward over her quivering breasts, her trembling belly, focusing on her slightly bulging sex. One of the golden orbs slipped further downward, the weight of the second one only making it harder to hold, the wetness already evident on her slim thighs.

"Don't let it fall," he reminded her with a wicked grin. She groaned, straining to keep her muscles tight, closing her eyes with the effort. When she felt him clamping something onto her nipple, though, her eyes flew open again. "It will only sting for a moment." She groaned as he clamped the other one on, looking down at the chain that connected them. Her nipples burned and she arched, moaning, twisting away from the pain, feeling the orbs slipping.

"Aidon, please!" He wasn't touching her, no part of him pressed against her, and Persephone longed to feel something, just the lightest feather's brush of flesh.

Persephone nearly lost her hold on the two golden orbs when Tisi pounded on the heavy door. "You must come quickly! Hermes has breached the inner sanctum!"

They both heard another voice. "Hades! It's me!"

More pounding. Persephone looked down at Aidon, her eyes wide. He sighed, shaking his head and leaned in to kiss her navel. "Be right back—don't let them fall!" She groaned as he stalked over and cracked open the door.

"Hermes, make it quick," he said. "I'm in the middle of something here."

Hermes' voice became clearer. "It is imperative I speak to you, oh High Lord of Darkness."

Aidon snorted. "Don't flatter me, or yourself. What is it?"

"It's Demeter." Hermes tried to peek inside. Persephone kept seeing the top of his head appearing around Aidon's shoulder. "She's turned the entire planet into an ice dam and it's been that way for months. She refuses to allow spring again unless you release her daughter."

Persephone's heart raced at the sound of her mother's name. She had thought of her often since she had been here and had hoped the message she sent with Sisyphus had reached her. Now she knew it had never reached Demeter.

"I am not keeping her here against her will," Aidon said through gritted teeth.

"So let me see for myself." Hermes' head appeared around his shoulder again. "Let me talk to her. I need to tell Zeus something!"

"Let him in, Aidon," she called. He shrugged and swung the door open wide.

Hermes stood in the doorway for a moment, his mouth agape. She knew what it must look like. "Hi, Hermes!"

"Persephone!" Hermes looked back and forth between them, his wide white wings, almost twice the size of his body, opened as if about to take flight. "Are you okay?"

She smiled. "Never better."

"Hades, you're keeping her prisoner!" Hermes hissed, the wings on his ankles buzzing like hummingbirds. "Let this girl go home to her mother."

Aidon stalked over to the bed, crossing his arms over his chest. "Persephone, are you a prisoner here?"

She shook the restraints above her head. "I think the chains are throwing him off, Aidon."

He chuckled and mouthed, "Don't let them fall," with his back turned to Hermes.

Persephone looked to the small winged man, still straining to keep the orbs from slipping further down. "I'm no prisoner, I can assure you."

Hermes looked back and forth between them again, rubbing his forehead. "Hades, this is serious. Haven't you noticed the influx of the dead? Thanatos said he tried to tell you! Mortals are dying, crops are failing, people are starving!"

Persephone frowned, remembering a whispered conversation between her husband and the God of Death. She had noticed the numbers of shades increasing and had wondered at it. "This is my mother's doing?"

"None other." Hermes settled himself into a large, dark chair in the corner. "She has been wandering day and night, wailing and mourning and looking for you. She told Zeus if you come home, she will bring spring back to the mortal world."

For a moment, Persephone let a wave of guilt and remorse wash over her. She felt small and young again, her mother's daughter, not the Queen of the Underworld.

"And if I don't?" she asked.

Hermes shrugged. "Then the big chill up there goes on indefinitely. Hence Zeus sending me here to fetch you."

Aidon stood, his eyes closed, head down. "Sephie, you need to go home."

"I am home," she said, her eyes flashing at him.

Hermes sat forward in the chair. "Look, there has to be some compromise we can come to here. Something that will make everyone happy."

"I'm not leaving my husband!" Persephone gritted her teeth, wincing and tightening everything below the waist as the orbs began to slip with the force of her words.

"Sephie, I know Demeter well." Aidon sighed. "She means to do what she says. If you do not go, she will cause the death of every mortal on the planet. Our gates will be overrun. I've been told about it, but I didn't want to tell you."

"Like I said," Hermes leaned forward, plucking a ripe, red apple from a bowl on the table beside him. "We have to think of a compromise."

"Do you want to get rid of me?" Persephone felt tears stinging her eyes.

"NO!" Aidon turned and grabbed the apple from Hermes hand, throwing it against the door where it splattered into pulp. He stood there, breathing hard for a moment. Then he looked at Hermes. "You know better, my friend. If you eat anything in the Underworld, you must stay here."

Persephone brightened. "I have eaten here!"

Hermes' face turned as white as his wings. "Uh-oh."

"I know." Aidon began to pace. They watched him padding back and forth like some dark beast.

"What should I tell Zeus?" Hermes asked.

"Zeus gave her to me!" Aidon growled, frowning, but not slowing his pace.

Persephone felt her tears slipping down her cheeks. "I don't want to leave you."

Aidon stopped. He looked at her for a moment, pained, and then closed his eyes.

"You decide, Sephie."

She looked between them, frowning. *Have I made a mistake, not telling my mother where I am?* Demeter had been wandering for months looking for her, agonizing over her disappearance. *If I'd just been a grown-up, and stood up for myself from the beginning...* She wondered if it would have made a difference, if she had taken Hecate up on her offer to send her mother a message. *It doesn't matter. I have the chance to be an adult—a queen—now.*

"Tell Demeter I have eaten in the Underworld, and by law, I must stay."

Aidon's eyes softened in relief. "Thank the gods!"

"Tell her that I ate six pomegranate seeds," Persephone said, her voice soft now. Aidon looked up at her, startled. "And for those six seeds, I must do penance here in the Underworld. For the other six months of the year, I will belong to my mother's world."

Hermes smiled. "See! Compromise! That's what I'm talking about."

"This can't be happening," Persephone whispered, her tear-filled eyes meeting Aidon's.

"It is a just and balanced decision." Aidon gave her a sad smile.

Hermes stood, frowning. "Should I take her with me?"

Aidon nodded, his voice hoarse. "Yes. I will release her to you later this day."

Persephone hung her head in defeat.

"Leave us," Aidon nodded at Hermes. "I will bring her to the gates."

Hermes fluttered to the door, and Persephone noticed his feet never really touched the ground. "I'm sorry," he said, looking over his shoulder at her, his face sad. She just shook her head, and then the messenger disappeared.

"Aidon, I don't think I can leave you," she cried. "I can't imagine being without you for six days, let alone six months!"

"I know, I know." He came to her, running his hand through her long hair. "But I can make it easier for you," he whispered, tracing the line of her lips with his finger.

"How?"

"Trust me," he murmured, standing in front of her bound form.

She smiled. "I do."

"I know." He returned her smile. "You never even let them fall."

"I wouldn't." She shook her head. "Unless you told me."

"Give it to me." Cupping his hand underneath her sex, but still not touching her, he waited. "Just one of them."

She slowly let her muscles go, releasing them bit by bit. The weight of the vibrating balls pressing down inside of her, coupled with her slick juices, made it nearly impossible not to let them both drop out of her at once. The first orb slipped through her swollen lips and plopped into Aidon's waiting hand. She moaned softly, gritting her teeth and pulling the other one up inside of her with all of her strength. The aching hum increased the moment she tightened her muscles, sending shockwaves of pleasure through her pelvis.

Aidon smiled. "Very good, Sephie." She squirmed, his praise filling her with almost as much heat as the vibrating object between her legs. "Now, give me the other one." She whimpered her assent, letting her muscles relax and the ball drop down to the opening of her sex. It hummed deliciously there, sending sweet thrills through her body, and she was loath to press it out, now. He saw her reluctance and smiled. "Do what I ask of you."

She sighed, bearing down just slightly and easing the orb out into his hand. He held them both up for her to see, the golden surface of each wet with her juices. They hummed in his fingers and she watched, fascinated, as he began to shift them, around and around. It required a deft touch, but he was clearly skilled, the balls switching places in his fingers so quickly she could barely tell them apart.

His hand drew closer to her sex, the balls flashing back and forth, and she gasped when he touched them to her aching omi at the top of her slit. His quick, dexterous movements made the pulsing balls rotate there, circling that throbbing nub of flesh.

"Oh, Aidon..." Her voice was just a breath and she arched her hips forward, the rising vibration between her legs growing with every quick movement of his hands. The balls orbited the sensitive, hooded swell of flesh she had been aching to touch for what seemed like hours. He gave her more pleasure than she had ever believed possible.

"Let it come, Persephone." His breath moved hot against her breasts and his tongue flicked over one of her nipples, making her moan. "Let it—"

As if his words had given her permission, she felt her pleasure peak at that moment. He pushed her to even greater heights, the thrilling rotation between her legs forcing her to buck and shudder in the restraints. The wave seemed to crest forever as she thrashed and pitched forward and back in her chains, her cries echoing through the room. Spent at last, she collapsed, ignoring the pain in her arms as her own weight pulled them taut.

Aidon caught her with one arm, tossing the balls next to her and unfastening her wrists with one hand before easing her back onto the bed. Still breathless, she turned her half-closed eyes to him, watching as he attached her arms to the other bedposts, pulling them tight enough to keep her arms spread above her head as she reclined on the bed. She didn't care what he did to her, anymore. He could beat her, brand her, tie her up—it didn't matter. The way he looked at her, touched her…somehow he made her into something she had longed to be and never knew she had even wanted.

He kissed her cheek, her forehead, the tips of her breasts. "Before you leave, you will swim in the Pool of Lethe."

Persephone shook her head. "The pool of forgetfulness? Why?"

"It's painful for the living to remember the dead." His voice cracked and he looked away from her.

"No," she whispered. "You will be dead to me."

He held her hand and kissed her fingertips. "Only for six months. For those six months you will be the Goddess of Spring again in your mother's arms."

"How will I know to come back?"

He kissed her, his mouth possessing hers. "I will come for you." She lost herself in the feel of his tongue, his hands in her hair. "And when you come home, you will swim in the pool of Mnemosyne."

"But then...we have to do this...all over again?" A smile dawned on her face as she remembered their first glorious night together.

"Yes." He kissed her neck. "I will do everything in my power to help you remember."

She felt tears slipping down her temples. "Then I will do what you ask of me."

He pulled her to him and she tried not to remember she was going—that for six months she would be without him. He kissed her and she forgot her mother, springtime, everything but the delicious coupling of their bodies. She let go of knowing she would have a lifetime of forgetting and remembering, an eternity of light and dark, of renewal and discovery. She forgot, and she was free.

The End

Pronunciation Key

Aeacus (Eye-ACK-us)
Aegina (Uh-GYNE-uh)
Aethra (Ay-EH-thra)
Aidon (AY-den)
Aidoneus (AY-duh-noose)
Alecto (Uh-LEC-toe)
Althaia (Al-THIGH-uh)
Aphrodite (Af-ro-DIGHT-ee)
Argonaut (AR-go-naught)
Artemis (AR-tuh-miss)
Asphodel (ASH-fo-del)
Atalanta (At-uh-LAN-tuh)
Athena (Uh-THEE-nuh)
Atropos (AT-row-pose)
Cerberus (SIR-burr-us)
Charon (CAR-on)
Cleopatra (Clee-oh-PAT-ruh)
Clotho (KLO-tho)
Demeter (DEH-muh-ter)
Diopeithes (Die-OP-uh-thees)
Discordia (Dis-CORD-ee-uh)
Elysium (Uh-LEE-see-um)
Erinyes (Uh-REN-yees)
Hecate (HECK-uh-tay)
Hephaestus (Huh-FESS-tus)
Hera (HAIR-uh)
Hermes (HER-mees)
Hippodamia (Hip-oh-DOM-ee-uh)
Hypnos (HIP-nose)
Ker (Care)
Keres (CARE-ees)
Kometes (Kuh-MEET-ees)
Lachesis (La-KEYS-iss)
Lapiths (LAP-iths)
Leda (LEE-duh)
Lethe (LETH-ee)

Megaera (Meg-EAR-uh)
Meleager (Mel-YA-ger)
Minos (ME-nos) Judge in the Underworld
Minthe (MIN-thee)
Miseria (Mis-AIR-ee-uh)
Mnemosyne (Nem-AH-sone-ay)
Moirai (MWAR-i)
Noire (NWAR-ay)
Omi (OH-me)
Omphalos (Ahm-FAL-ohs)
Persephone (Per-SEH-fone-ee)
Petulantia (Pet-u-LAHN-tee-uh)
Pirithous (Per-ITH-oo-us)
Polydeuces (Poly-DO-cheez)
Prothous (PRO-thoo-us)
Rhadamanthus (Rahd-uh-MAHN-thus)
Sephie (SEF-ee)
Styx (Sticks)
Sisyphus (SIS-uh-fuss)
Tartarus (TAR-tar-us)
Thanatos (THAN-uh-toes)
Theseus (THEE-see-us)
Thestios (THESS-tee-ohs)
Tisi (TEE.See)
Tisiphone (Tis-SEH-fone-ee)
Zeus (Zoos)

The End

ABOUT SELENA KITT

Like any feline, Selena Kitt loves the things that make her purr-and wants nothing more than to make others purr right along with her! Pleasure is her middle name, whether it's a short cat nap stretched out in the sun or a long kitty bath. She makes it a priority to explore all the delightful distractions she can find, and follow her vivid and often racy imagination wherever it wants to lead her.

Her writing embodies everything from the spicy to the scandalous, but watch out-this kitty also has sharp claws and her stories often include intriguing edges and twists that take readers to new, thought-provoking depths.

When she's not pawing away at her keyboard, Selena runs an innovative publishing company (www.excessica.com) and in her spare time, she devotes herself to her family—a husband and four children— and her growing organic garden. She also loves bellydancing and photography.

Her books *EcoErotica* (2009), *The Real Mother Goose* (2010) and *Heidi and the Kaiser* (2011) were all Epic Award Finalists. Her only gay male romance, *Second Chance*, won the Epic Award in Erotica in 2011. Her story, *Connections*, was one of the runners-up for the 2006 Rauxa Prize, given annually to an erotic short story of "exceptional literary quality," out of over 1,000 nominees, where awards are judged by a select jury and all entries are read "blind" (without author's name available.)

She can be reached on her website at
www.selenakitt.com

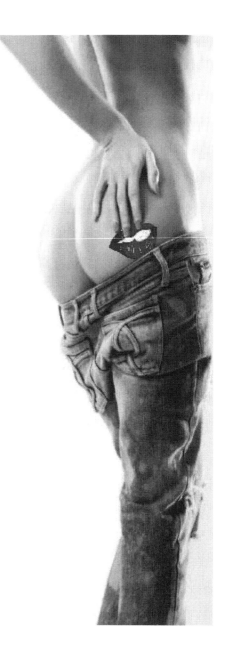